HARPER

A COLLECTION OF
HORRORS

GUNNAR K. A. NJALSSON

SPACEPOL

HARPER
A COLLECTION OF
HORRORS

GUNNAR K. A. NJALSSON

HARPER
A COLLECTION OF
HORRORS

SPACEPOL

First published 2018 in the Republic of Estonia
Cover: G. N. Chandler Graafika Baltic

British Library Cataloguing in Publication Data.
A catalogue record for this book is available from the British Library.

ISBN-13: 9781987881011

To my father.

◤ TABLE OF CONTENTS ◢
▼◁

1

MY CONFESSION

I f I had abided by the advice and listened to the pleadings – even threats – of family and friends, this book would never have seen the light of day. My mother accuses me of wanting to proliferate the nearly constant nightmares everyone in my family has – including my own night terrors – to the rest of the world. She says I am trying to afflict unsullied people who know nothing about Harper or its many dark moments. Why? Because they *don't* have the memories and the nightmares. Other people have "normal" problems and concerns. In other words, it's a classic case of "misery loves company". Since neither my family nor I nor most who lived in Harper between 1950 and 1980 will ever be "normal" or have "normal" problems, I am trying to spread our horror and trepidation to the rest of humanity. That's how my mother describes my motive for putting this all down in writing.

But that's not my objective. I want to acknowledge what I know and to come clean about Harper. If my mother and sister, my cousins, old school friends or other former residents of that southern California city want to act like nothing happened and keep silent, then I wish them well. They all share the same superstition about discussing this topic – that the "things from Harper", as they refer to them, will come back and finish what they started decades ago.

Their fears of reprisal sound like something straight out of a Stephen King novel. Harper, California is not Derry, Maine. An evil shapeshifting clown is not going to show up and I am not attempting to gather a group of former Harperites to come back and take on the evil. In fact, none of us even know what we were dealing with back then. No motives were explained, and no demands were made. The government doesn't even seem to know. It could all have been a manifestation of biology or physics unknown to the world decades ago and still largely a mystery even today. I don't know if these things were evil. But the incidents certainly weren't good for anyone involved, including those of us who survived.

I wish Harper were that fictional town. For then it would be good entertainment with a plot and a point; not real enough to make grown men and women – including policemen and FBI agents – cower and piss their pants like small children when they recall it, even when they've not set foot near the city for more than thirty years.

If Harper were a city from a horror novel, we would have at least a chance of knowing what we were dealing with – something exotic but graspable. However, as you will see, that's not the case with Harper.

No. I'm writing this because I am sick to death of the fear, the reticence and the denial on the part of government and former residents. The victims who can't speak need a voice. What happened to them should not be neatly swept away because it doesn't fit in with our insatiable craving for an ordered world with motives, cause and effect.

These were living people – children and families – living their lives and doing the best they could. Their normal lives were swept away by something so horrible and surreal that nobody wants to even acknowledge it. And when they were gone a part of the rest of us went with them.

Those of us who got away owe it to them to be as brutal in our honesty as the fates which these victims met and to let the world know that there *are* monsters! There *are* menaces which we haven't even begun to study or comprehend!

So here I offer my confession, the truth Harperites don't want to deal with: there are unknown beings that actually enjoy taunting and doing horrific things to humans just for the fun of it, because they can! There doesn't have to be a motive, a plan or any reason at all. For reasons unknown, Harper has been a rallying point of sorts for these beings or "things" where they could focus their deadly handiwork on humanity. Harper is *not* normal and many of us who live or lived there are *not* normal!

As I write these words, the watery precursors to tears fill a pair of jaded and cynical grey eyes which haven't shed any tears for a very long time. If I am in fact now crying, I am doing so for those who are no longer with us. But I am also crying for me. What a contemptable coward I have been for all of these years, keeping all of this inside of me just like the others do. Every paragraph that fills these pages constitutes a triumphant coup against that denial!

Candidly, I have no idea where to start this morbid exposé or how to organize it. Amidst being threatened with privacy invasion lawsuits or being reported to the police by the County History Consortium, it was all I could do to even try to gather specific names and information. For so long, I have been living with these horrors and fighting with family and with the Consortium to even risk telling these stories that I hadn't had time to even plan the presentation.

Do I lay out the terror and loss of life in chronological order? Should I relate the more palatable and less ghastly horrors first, allowing the reader to gradually develop an immunity of sorts to the repulsion, fright and panic?

There is no emotionally polite or psychologically sanitized way to tell this story. So I have settled on what for me is the only option if I do not want to end up again in psychiatric treatment. I will start with what I can deal with emotionally and take it from there. I will work from what my own family has recounted to me to what I personally experienced in the 1970's.

Then, I will reluctantly try to recall the horrific news and grisly gossip my mother and father would discuss late at night when they thought I was sleeping and while they alternated between shouting matches, worrying and whining with intermittent bouts of re-checking the locks on each window and door – as if that would have helped anything. As a child I heard and understood much more than my parents would like to believe. But in hindsight I can hardly blame them for at least trying to preserve my childhood innocence before I too was finally exposed to true terror.

If there are sceptics out there reading this and who are intent on declaring these events "science fiction", "hogwash" or "legend" please bring on your science, research teams, methods and your alternate logical explanations. There are thousands of people who would do anything – and I mean *anything* – to have you prove that there are natural explanations for the events that have scarred our lives and taken away friends and loved ones. Perhaps then we would know how to prevent them from recurring in the future.

I read while in college in Argentina that monsters are creations we don't yet understand, that the supernatural is simply physics that we have yet to fathom. Now that I shall finally lay out this horrendous and bizarre spectacle for your critical viewing, please do offer your erudite, rational and mundane explanations.

You will find that some current and former Harperites have a profound need to make sense of the more than three decades of irrational, bizarre and senseless terror that plagued our growing town. Most, however, just want to forget and move on, to return to a simple world and to the belief that the delinquency of our follow humans is all that we really have to fear. Those who experienced what we did know that nothing could be further from the truth.

2

HARPER: GEOLOGY AND AN UNSETTLING HISTORY
1860-1979

I n the late 1800's the mesa that Harper now occupies was grazing land which had only recently been ceded from Mexico to the United States of America along with the rest of the state which had been called Alta California or Upper California. Everyone has heard about the California Gold Rush and many know of the numerous estancias that dotted the early California countryside – especially in southern California. The fact that California sits on both major and minor faults is also common knowledge. Some astute citizens even know that new faults are still being discovered – even in southern California.

To say that Harper sits right atop a very ancient and very deep fault in the earth's crust would probably frighten someone looking for prime real estate. But geologists are quick to reassure wary residents and buyers alike that few if any of these smaller ancient faults would play a major role in any conceivable earthquake. That removes at least one risk from the list. It still doesn't put to rest the concerns that one geologist had about the Translucene Fault upon which Harper sits.

Dr. Avery Gohrn – a 59-year-old somewhat eccentric senior geologist from the US Geological Survey office in San Francisco – was on the scene before Huntingdon, Newland Beach, Daughn or Harper began to grow and thrive. He arrived in the county with the task of improving soil classification maps and locating possible mineral or oil fields using the new technologies and better methods of his day. This was when the first orange groves which dotted the tablelands near the sea had only recently begun to bear fruit.

Dr. Gohrn could be seen almost daily moving from location to location, conducting heavy equipment drivers and telling them where to sink drills and ground probes into the earth. Some days he was collecting surface soil samples at the edge of the ocean and inadvertently filling his formerly stylish brown dress shoes with off-white beach sand as he absentmindedly traipsed toward the darker, firmer sand that was hurriedly expelling seawater as the waves receded. Another day he would set up his team and bizarre-looking equipment on top of the Harper mesa a bit more inland from the Pacific Ocean – still with its own spectacular, unhindered view of the sea only some miles to the west.

The clean-shaven, six-foot-tall, sticklike figure with thinning light red hair and round, gold-rimmed glasses would take in short glimpses of Catalina Island which was thirty miles from the shore — a mountain top at the other side of a vast canyon submerged by a seemingly calm greenish blue sea. He could see it for the violent geological reminder that it was. His hired help could scarcely imagine it. To them Catalina Island was nothing more than a holiday destination with a casino one visited for weddings or parties, only to later have difficulty remembering what had gone on after sobering up — and this, despite alcohol prohibition.

In Dr. Gohrn's day deep diving missions into the channel between Catalina and the mainland were less a reality and more a topic for fantasy books. The San Pedro Shelf, a flat area of relatively shallow water, extends from Los Angeles all the way down to Newland Beach south of Huntingdon. Beyond this shelf to the west and south the floor drops abruptly to depths which were unreachable by divers contemporary to Dr. Gohrn. But the very limited depths to which divers could then descend brought tales of "cracks" and "caves" which continued from the canyon wall at the San Pedro Shelf's western edge eastward and perhaps even inland under Huntingdon and Harper.

Dr. Gohrn was the first to point out that a chasm or fracture, later found to be a minor fault, likely crossed from the area beneath the Huntingdon shoreline eastward and under the mesa where Harper is now located. The past months of research had begun to paint a picture — a sinister portrait of an unusually deep fissure perhaps less than three hundred feet below the surface in some places.

Now, with rock and sediment layers giving away beneath the bit of his diesel-powered rotary drill, he was as confused as he was intrigued to know that oil might be present in both Huntingdon and Harper. But whatever oil there was in the vicinity of the chasm seemed to "dry up" or disappear shortly after the drill broke through and locally shattered the sediment and rock layer capping the chasm. Was it possible that oil and groundwater were leaking into the chasm below? Dr. Gohrn often wondered. The fissure would have to be very deep, maybe thousands or tens of thousands of feet!

In what might today be called a very primitive attempt to measure seismic waves, Dr. Gohrn allowed an "electronic ground listening stethoscope" or microphone to be lowered via the vertical drilling pipe into the chasm. There is no information as to how far down the microphone was lowered or whether any of his co-workers were in on the listen.

The eccentric government geologist took an early retirement after this unorthodox experiments produced results which, when reported, led his supervisor and colleagues to seriously question Dr. Gohrn's sanity.

Whatever Dr. Gohrn heard or thought he heard alarmed him enough to make him recommend that all drilling – including for oil or natural gas – be forbidden anywhere near the Translucene Fault, meaning Huntingdon, Harper, Daughn and even Newland Beach. With the California oil industry constantly discovering new sources of oil wealth, the powers that be were not about to take Avery Gohrn's advice. He begged the oil companies and he begged the government. He begged them all, but to no avail.

Neither big oil nor state and federal government were going to listen to warnings like those put forth by Dr. Gohrn. Imaginations were certainly more fertile back then. It wasn't uncommon even for scientists to claim having found the "mouth of hell" or similar spectacles which hit the newspaper headlines and then died out just as quickly as they had become news. But even the journalists he trusted began to believe that Dr. Avery Gohrn was a highly educated and overpaid crackpot. They gave little credence to his warnings about an "unknown subterranean source of hair-raising sounds possibly responding to and alerted by now to the drilling and tests above".

Needless to say, Dr. Gohrn's career came to a rather abrupt halt together with all investigations of his "chasm". This is supposed to have occurred during the 1920's.

So the sprawling land of off-white beaches and light brown sandstone cliffs by the deep blue sea and miles of orange groves and berry farms on the coastal tablelands continued its development unabated into dozens of towns which later became cities. Oil drilling and discovery continued as well. Save for agriculture, the land was open and had a scarcity of greenery or trees. The tablelands barely two miles from the seashore gave way to rolling hills to the south and east which were green with grass during the winter and spring – yellow during the rest of the year. Even further inland, the rolling hills gradually met jutting mountains off in the distance fifty to one hundred and fifty miles to the north and east.

This relatively low coastal basin wedged between the sea and minor mountains had a Mediterranean climate with its rainy season in the winter. Most days were sunny and the sky was often a striking pure blue. In the fall and winter the morning sunlight bathed the tablelands and rolling hills in a hue as red as wine.

In the summer a fog of sorts obscured the blue sky for the early hours of the day and retreated westward some miles out to sea as the day progressed. There the clouds and fog lay in wait, allowing coastal towns and sunbathers on the beaches to have their share of carefree sunshine before the clouds again made landfall once the sun had set – sometimes even before it had set.

In the 1940's citrus groves began to slowly surrender their space to military barracks, airstrips, roads and even a small railway. After WWII military buildings were moved or converted for civilian purposes and conscripts stayed on with their families as simple single family houses and bungalows were constructed in record time alongside the various streets which were straight and arranged in a north-south and east-west grid like pattern.

One of the westernmost of these mass-produced one-story, single family housing projects was the Patriot Palaces neighborhood which was at the westernmost edge of the tablelands right where the wall of sandstone cliffs descended westward to the lowlands and the long Huntingdon shoreline. All of this was built over the former Kearns airstrip and barracks facility where bomber aircraft in transit between Hawaii and the eastern US landed and were serviced during the 1930's and 1940's. And this is also the point in time where Harper history starts to get more interesting.

There had been so many accidents and deaths here during the very short time the airstrip was in use that a five-star air force general had intervened directly and arranged the closure of Kearns – not just its closure; its complete obliteration! Anyone familiar with the process for decommissioning of military facilities knows that normally this is a long and formal process. Kearns airstrip and barracks were virtually abandoned before any final decision about decommissioning was made.

Essentially, no one wanted to work there and pilots used other nearby airfields while tending to avoid Kearns due to its reputation as an accident-prone airstrip where five fatal plane accidents had already taken place in just ten years.

That's not counting five deaths and two near-deaths caused by a mess hall cook who decided one slow afternoon in March of 1946 to lace the coffee with hydrofluoric acid. Those who liked their coffee black drank up, while those who used cream or milk immediately noticed something strange. The unfortunate officers who ingested the corrosive chemical were discretely, one-by-one pulled by the cook into the kitchen where they lay on the floor agonizing and vomiting out pieces of their throats and stomachs.

That is, until the cook came back to attend to each one by force-feeding the men melted plastic. The men were then "stored" in a utility closet and the stench of melted plastic, blood and burnt flesh in that kitchen is said to have driven one responding medic to later commit suicide after years of unsuccessful psychiatric treatment.

Still more sinister is the fact that the "cook" who was described by witnesses as an older man, having a greyish hue and with "unusually narrow, yellowish eyes like a liver patient" couldn't be identified as anyone who had ever worked at the facility and he had basically disappeared into thin air by the time personnel were mobilized to investigate. The apparent imposter cook's

14

almost surreal and unnerving appearance had been enough to send some officers into town for their lunch and coffee instead of using the services of the mess hall. The cook who officially *did* work there had called in sick with presumed food poisoning two days earlier and the mess hall was supposed to be closed for lack of personnel.

For reasons which should now be apparent, you won't find much about Kearns airstrip and barracks in the official history of Harper. A cousin of mine who volunteered at the History Consortium stumbled by accident upon the Kearns documentation, which was to be found in a "private archive" donated to the Consortium by a former military police who had worked at Kearns. When my cousin asked about the documents one day at a Consortium meeting she was soon thereafter pulled aside and politely told that her services as a volunteer were no longer required. That was in 1963.

Not much else is known about the abrupt decommissioning of Kearns, save that all buildings were levelled to the ground and the airstrip covered with massive amounts of gravel and dirt. Then the developers were quickly brought in to work their transformational magic, and by 1954 Patriot Palaces stood where the seemingly cursed Kearns had once operated.

In fact, anyone not from the area would never know Kearns had even existed by looking at the neat rows of houses and newly planted trees. The only sign of the former airstrip itself is a shallow terrace or embankment that runs along the property lines in the backyards of the rows of houses on the west side of Ballistic Avenue and east side of Liberia Avenue.

While west Harper pays no specific tribute to Kearns, it does commemorate the former military nature of the area through street names like Shell Shock Avenue, Shrapnel Street or Mercy Shot Boulevard – the bustling, wide thoroughfare which divides the city of Harper into separate west and east sections. There have been political fights about the appropriateness of these street names on and off since the late 1960's, but nothing substantial has come of it.

Nonetheless, some streets on the west side have toned down their military fervor with name changes during the 1970's. For instance, Christ Almighty Elementary – the private school once attended by my sister and I – is located on March Street. The name was changed to "March! Street" in 1972 from "General Pershing Sir! Street" due to postal confusion and new spelling guidelines for street and place names. The exclamation mark was eventually dropped for the same reason in 1981.

The tiny enclave city of Daughn is only reachable via Oaf Street which runs right from Liberia Avenue due west toward Huntingdon over the city line and down a steep hill lined with very large old oak, pine and Siberian larch trees. Daughn was separated from Harper in 1949 and planned so as to be "a piece of Europe" in the new county, which had itself been separated from Los Angeles. Oaf Street becomes Ave Daughn once inside the chic satellite city which has no road access to Huntingdon, even though it sits partially within this beach city. Palm trees, cacti or indeed nearly any type of vegetation typical of southern California gardens are forbidden by the ultra-strict city code. Street names have to "sound exotic and European", like Ave Roentgen, Blvd Amiralteyski or Place Débussy.

Daughn, just like Harper from which it sprang, has had its share of terrible events. Yet, few of them have involved monsters or ghosts. Most have consisted of murderous feuds between the rich Russian and Italian émigré families living there and the occasional fatal attempt by corrupt council members to cover up misappropriation of city funds.

The freak death of the fourth mayor of Daughn – Mr. Alexandr Antoinello Mancini – in 1962 is the exception. It is said that Mr. Mancini was the last truly honest and accountable mayor of Daughn. Sadly, that era in Daughn's history ended one May afternoon as the rather dull and pedantic ex-accountant who was known for being quite committed to home and family life made the fatal mistake of mowing his backyard lawn.

Just over the light brown picket fence a head of backcombed, salt and pepper hair could be seen going to and fro. Two slits for eyes behind the square glasses and an upside down triangle for a mouth gave Mr. Mancini the near expressionless look which, for anyone who met him, only served to confirm stereotypes of persons with his previous profession. Maude Mancini, his wife, was inside the house in the kitchen quickly washing, rinsing and drying dishes and coffee cups to prepare for their customary Thursday evening guests for a game of bridge. Their two daughters were sitting in the living room finishing their school work before going out for their customary Thursday evening roller-skating dates.

As Mr. Mancini turned and began to push his green De Luxe self-propelled lawnmower forward for what must have been the tenth or eleventh of his neat and systematic passes over the backyard lawn, he felt a slight rumble in the ground below him. Curious and confused, he stopped for a moment intending to shut off the mower and listen or check the area where he felt the strange movement. He never got that far.

Hardly a moment after the thought entered his mind he felt the familiar sensation of being in an elevator quickly descending to a lower floor. The sound of the lawnmower rocketed in less than two seconds from just in front of his feet to eye level. When he instantly and reflexively grabbed hold of the ledge of the hole that was opening up beneath him and stopped his freefall, the deafening drone of the infernal machine was nearly just

18

above his head. He couldn't even hear the tons of earth falling into the pitch black void beneath his dangling feet.

Maude had seen the entire event from the kitchen window. Initially she had stood idly by in disbelief, her mouth open and eyes staring blankly ahead as if all of these things were happening on a television screen and had nothing to do with her husband in their backyard. But they did, and it finally registered for her that this bizarre scene was real. It was happening now! Her husband had in fact only seconds earlier stood normally above ground behind the lawnmower. His legs, torso and much of his lower head had in fact quickly shot downward and been hidden by the neat and tidy green lawn almost instantaneously. And now her husband was hanging on for dear life as the lawn and ground in front of him began to sag downward causing the lawnmower to begin to roll backward.

Maude Mancini tossed dish, rag and apron onto the kitchen counter and screamed "Girls! Your father!" as she struggled with the door in the kitchen that led directly to their backyard. Mrs. Androwskiy, the Mancinis' next-door neighbor, had also seen the mayor almost disappear into the ground as she went to move their swirly-boy lawn sprinkler to its next position on her plush, green backyard lawn. Luckily, so many eyes had witnessed the bizarre fate of Mr. Mancini. That luck, though, quickly turned to something else as Mrs. Androwskiy ran into the Mancinis' house and followed the two daughters who had followed their mother to the backyard through the kitchen door.

"Hose! Get the hose!" Mr. Mancini had tried to yell exasperated as the insanely loud mower drowned out his voice. Finally, he did something he should not have done. He lifted his right arm which had clutched a tuft of grass and motioned toward the garden hose which was neatly coiled and hanging from its holder against the house wall. Mrs. Mancini turned her head so fast that her teased hairdo with a headband holding back her dark brown hair at the crown could barely keep up. Her large blue eyes widened even further and she started jerking large sections of the garden hose free from the holder. It was ultimately all for naught.

As the daughters and neighbor lady stood cautiously away from the unstable fissure and sagging lawn, Mr. Mancini again felt that fatal, ultra-low rumble which had put him where he now was. The ground began once again to give way and the lawn sagged even more causing the lawnmower to nearly tip over backwards as it picked up speed and made its final journey toward the top of Mr. Mancini's head.

Only two weeks earlier, Mr. Mancini had taken the lawnmower in to Chief's Garden Tools in Harper to have the oil changed and the blades sharpened. Perhaps that slightly lessened his agony as the mower rolled backward chopping off one of the mayor's fingers and ultimately making a sickening, hollow popping sound as it severed the top of his skull and spit it out some yards away where it then landed neatly in the Mancini family's tomato garden, next to the picket fence.

Having completed its final morbid assignment the infernal mower sank together with an already dead Mr. Mancini to its rightful resting place in the bowels of the earth. The sound of the motor became all the more muffled and finally ceased as the earth near the now much larger hole turned and sank. Half of the Mancinis' backyard was now a hole at least a hundred feet deep, perhaps more.

The only sign of mercy shown by the forces behind the sordid fate of the last honest mayor of Daughn was the fact that the severed finger, now laying close to the uncoiled garden hose was still − just barely − wearing Mr. Mancini's wedding ring.

Even deep holes can eventually be filled up and sealed. But nothing about Daughn has been quite the way it was since then and Mrs. Mancini was in and out of psychiatric care until 1989 when she passed away. The daughters moved out of state a couple of years after the incident and never even came for their mother's funeral. They and their families are currently involved in a bitter dispute over their inheritance as their mother left everything to Daughn's only cathedral − the Russian Orthodox St. Nicholas Church of Daughn attended by nearly eighty percent of the inhabitants.

Perhaps it is this scarred mentality which in some macabre way unites the inhabitants of Daughn and Harper. It would then be the only thing in common between the citizens of these two very different communities who hardly even speak to one another. If Harper had been spared so as to have only one such ghoulish incident like that of Daughn, the city's inhabitants would have much to be thankful for. But that's not the case.

⋙ ⋘ ⋙

Even the yearly city theme park carnival of Harper – Tivoli Days – has not been spared. Since 1949 the city of Harper has sponsored a yearly summer event with carnival rides, performances, a baby contest and an all-you-can-eat hamburger buffet. And it is always held in May and always in Tivoli Park on the corner of 12th Street and Librarian Avenue. Mrs. Kariis, who owned a secondhand bookshop on the corner of Mercy Shot and 12th Street, detested the event almost from its inception, as Tivoli Park was just across the street from her bookstore.

From the 1960's onward, rock music from successive generations would blare across several blocks mixed with the near rhythmic screaming of youngsters riding the wildest rides. Irritated, Mrs. Kariis would frequently glance over the top of her oval, bifocal eyeglasses out the store window toward Tivoli Park exposing her unusually bushy black and grey eyebrows together with her utter disapproval as she shook her head and went back to sorting newly arrived books.

Some years of suffering through the four days of noise, crowds and unkempt carnival workers asking to use her restroom were unlike others. The first of these years was 1976 when two of the cars from the "Whiplash" ride were thrown clear and flew into another ride called the "Zipper", which tilted and fell over while in motion.

While talking to a frequent customer about the constant noise coming from the park, their discussion halted abruptly when a very unexpected and unsettling voice echoed their way from Tivoli Park across the street asking in an almost effeminate, soft tone over the ride's loudspeaker, "Do ya wanna go faster and die?" Apparently, most hadn't given the words any thought and the usual unison response of those on the whiplash ride was an overwhelming "Yes!!" Whoever or whatever was now running the ride kept their grim promise and jettisoned two of the carts by means still to this day under debate.

Mrs. Kariis and her faithful customer managed just in time to witness the Zipper lean in an odd direction and then disappear from sight below the other rides, followed by wilder screaming than usual and crying. The festive music eventually stopped, and ambulances and fire department arrived together with the police.

There were also the Ghost Train electrocutions where passengers had been doused with cold water and thrown from their carts onto the electrified tracks inside the pitch black ride. Three people died this way in both 1977 and 1978. The Whiplash incident in 1976 took five lives- the most ever for Harper's Tivoli Days carnival.

Arrests were made, but even those victims who survived and recovered their memories denied that those arrested had anything to do with the incidents.

The suspect some of them did describe was chalked up to their shock, horror and bad nerves after the incidents. After all, this was a carnival and not a circus sideshow. No bug-eyed werewolf monster with a crew cut and dishwater blonde hair all over its face was or had ever been employed by the carnival ride company.

As much as she hated the Tivoli Days carnival, Mrs. Kariis was not glad about these events and particularly not about the bloodcurdling voice she and her customer had heard that May afternoon in 1976. In fact, she often wondered whether whoever was responsible could have been someone from the carnival who had previously used her bookstore restroom. Had she perhaps come face-to-face with a highly intelligent and crafty mass murderer?

Mrs. Hanson – the feisty and red-haired sixty year old who ran her own dry cleaning shop on 13th street near the intersection with Shrapnel – had heard the chilling

24

tale from Mrs. Kariis' customer who was there. It was Mrs. Hanson who christened the suspected saboteur and super killer the "wolf man thing from Tivoli Park".

"You know, if it's true, then the wolf man thing has knocked off at least eight people, gotten away with murder, in public, eight times!" Mrs. Hanson would exclaim to customers such as my maternal grandparents in the 1970's.

She had other stories to tell her customers as well, as she had lived in Harper almost since the city was founded – even longer than my family who had showed up in Harper in 1954.

They came south to the new county from Los Angeles. My sister had been born in that city in 1954 just as my mother herself had been. But my grandparents were not from there. My grandfather had come from Estonia which was then part of the Russian Empire. He was born there on October 10th 1897 and came with his cousins to Connecticut in the US in 1917 when he was only 19 years old. His name was Charles W. Ahnus. I don't know what the "W" stands for and I don't like the last name, because it sounds like "anus" or at least people sometimes pronounce it that way. Most people try to avoid the trap and politely pronounce it "anise" like the exotic spice. Grandfather's family surname is supposed to be very noble – at least in Europe. So he always told us to be proud and not ashamed of that name.

My grandfather married my grandmother – Virginia A Ruth – just five years after he came to the United States. She was born in Kentucky in October 1898. My mother – Leida B. Ahnus – was then born in Los Angeles on November 8th 1934. She married my father there in 1952. My father – Gareth Groff – was born in Los Angeles in 1927.

Then, November 11th, 1965, I was born as Gordon Nathan Groff – the second child and only son born to my parents. The family moved to Harper just as the Patriot Palaces homes were being completed, and they moved in to a fresh single family home with four bedrooms and two baths at the corner of Ballistic Avenue and 14th Street which runs east and west.

For a short time – less than two years – both my parents and my mother's parents, along with my sister Marina Groff who was born in 1954, lived in that four-bedroom house atop a little embankment which is part of the remnant of what was once Kearns airstrip. Down this little hill behind the backyard is another house much like my grandparents' home. In fact, it is almost a copy. They bought this neighboring property in 1956 so that my mother and father could have their own home for their family.

That is the home my parents lived in when I was born- a one-story single family home and garage located on the corner of 14th Street and Liberia Avenue in the Patriot Palaces neighborhood of Harper. Other family members bought similar houses in this same neighborhood and moved down from Los Angeles so that we could all be close together.

The oleander bushes beside our garage had not yet been planted. The cherry tree next to the driveway was less than four feet high. Grandmother's and Grandfather's rubber tree was a small indoor plant in a pot and hadn't yet been planted in the corner of their backyard where my sister and I used to play.

In 1957 my grandfather received a pleasant surprise when he saw new people moving in to the house next to his on Ballistic and the father with short, strawberry blonde hair was speaking a language my grandfather hadn't heard since he was very young. These were their new neighbors – the Tamms. Mr. Priit Tamm, grandfather's new neighbor was speaking Estonian and they immediately hit it off and talked for hours. Grandfather and my father helped the Tamms move in to their new home and soon the Tamms' home was an extension of our own which had previously only consisted of the two houses we owned.

Esther, Mr. Tamm's wife, was a forgetful but active homemaker who wore her heart on her sleeve and who my sister and I could always trust to cry when we told her about something that had hurt us. It is said that her hair used to be jet black, but no one in my family could remember it being anything other than dark grey. Esther

Tamm had big, baroque-style hair like the paintings you see of the composer Georg Friedrich Händel. And this was before big hair became popular in the 1970's.

My sister became a virtual sister to Trisha Tamm, the Tamm's tomboy daughter who was two years older. Mr. and Mrs. Tamm had fled Soviet Estonia in 1946 via Sweden and then Canada. They then came as Cold War immigrants to the United States in 1952. Trisha had been born in Toronto, Canada. So she was technically Canadian. But for my sister, all of this was irrelevant banter that only Mrs. Tamm cared about.

My grandparents and the Tamms were friends as long as they lived; my sister and Trisha until Trisha moved far away from Harper. The only misunderstanding between our families came sometime in the late 1960's when three men in suits and bowties came over from the Tamms' house to talk to my grandparents, my mother, my sister and I about our Estonian roots. At the time none of us understood that there was actually a network of consulates of the formerly free Republic of Estonia keeping tabs on Estonian emigrants and potential citizens of the formerly free republic.

The Tamms had told them about my grandfather. They meant absolutely no harm, but my grandfather had his own ideas.

Once he understood who the men were and what they wanted, he quickly switched from Estonian and started cursing in English and drove them off down the driveway toward the street screaming "We're not any goddam foreigners; we're Americans, you goddamn sons of bitches!"

Neighbors out watering their lawns that evening got a short taste of the bizarre in this otherwise quiet neighborhood. That was the last contact we ever had with the exile Estonian consular system.

Eventually, fences were mended with the Tamms who were themselves generally very suspicious and afraid of any strangers who wanted information about their family, particularly those who spoke Estonian or Russian and who had recently moved to the US or Canada. Esther Tamm cried with relief when the short-lived, inter-family storm was over.

3

MARINA:
GOD HELP A LITTLE GIRL
1958

I f anything reveals a predator, it is the position and nature of the eyes. Gentle animals tend to have their eyes far apart or even on the sides of their heads. Their gaze is for the fields and plant life which they feed on and for staying close to the flock around them. For animals that live on land, the position of the eyes tells much. When eyes are set close together in the front of the head we have, almost without exception, a predator. Predator and prey are locked in a chase to the death. One is chasing the other, eyes focused and large, straight ahead. The other is only focused on staying alive for another moment while drenched in the cold and musk odor of fear, barely looking death in the whites of the eyes.

Such thoughts had never entered the mind of a four-year-old girl with brown locks of hair down to her shoulder blades as she whisked the pencil back and forth and completed coloring in the black ears of her favorite cartoon character. This was the latest coloring book her grandparents had bought for her and she was also practicing remembering the lines of the Mickey Mouse Club song before this evening's episode was scheduled to start. Marina Groff sat on the bed in the back bedroom of her grandparents' house on the corner of Ballistic Avenue and 14th Street in Harper, California. March 14th, 1958 is the exact date for those who care. My sister herself will never forget that date or its events for as long as she lives.

The headboard of the four-poster bed with no tester upon which she sat in her Cinderella ruffle lace pink and white dress was positioned against the south wall of a bedroom where she would sleep when staying with her grandparents. The walls were papered with geometric snowflake designs in pink, tan and maroon – wallpaper which she herself had picked out together with her grandfather some months earlier. Only an hour earlier the afternoon sun had been shining outside so intensely and brightly that she had no need for the ceiling lamp.

Now, the afternoon sun was causing the backyard outside the bedroom window next to the headboard to turn pink and then red. The shadows of the creosote wood fence between her grandparents' yard and the

Tamms' grew longer on the small cement sidewalk beside the house. Soon her favorite TV program would begin, but it was getting too dark to color pictures without the lights on. Marina's mother was down the hall in the living room at the other end of the house. The grandparents were in town running errands.

It was only when Marina hopped off the bed and reached for the light switch near the door leading to the dark hallway that she noticed she wasn't completely alone. She hesitated and didn't flip the switch which would have required her to stretch her arm as far as she could and then jump upward. Marina turned toward the window, straining to see whoever might have been observing her from outside.

Somebody was definitely outside in the yard, had just moved past the window and was walking around out there. She knew this to be so since she could feel each footstep the unknown visitor was taking and even hear the broad dresser mirror to the left of her rattling with each step the stranger took.

She assumed it must be a grownup. But neither Dad's nor Grandfather's footsteps were ever that heavy. The pounding footsteps hastened as the visitor once again passed by the bedroom window so fast that all Marina could make out was a big, black blur. So she edged closer to the window between the dresser and the bed, nervously and repetitively clutching the bottom of her little dress with her right hand. Her mother hadn't reacted to the visitor, and she didn't hear the voices of her grandparents in the front of the house. Now she began to realize that something was very, very wrong.

In what seemed like an instant, the light of late afternoon outside became even weaker than that of dusk, as though perhaps thick clouds had suddenly covered the sun. Everything was a dim grey, even the red tile roof of the Tamms' house just over the fence, which Marina strained for a moment to see. The entire house then shook as the view was instantly blocked in front of her.

A black, undefined mass now began to move slowly downward. But before she could even figure out what her brown eyes were looking at, a huge circle of condensation suddenly appeared on the outside of the window in front of her head.

For a few seconds that mist protected the long-haired, four-year-old girl in a short pink dress from seeing the ghastly face of what was looking directly at her from the other side of the thin pane of glass. But as she slowly backed away from the window in order to run out of the room and through the dark hall to her mother, the mist on the glass evaporated and she froze up.

The eyes!

Initially that was all she could make out from the enormous thing crouched down just outside the window and looking straight at her. The monolid, close-set eyes were so strikingly white, except for small blue irises and pupils, which were constricting and dilating as it examined Marina. In those eyes, which were now settling into a death gaze directed straight ahead at little Marina, she saw an evil which immobilized her and a pure hatred as ancient as time itself. She began to wet her pants.

The warm urine drizzled down her legs and turned cold as it reached her socks and she began to fully perceive the full face of this deadly fiend. The shiny black upper lip had begun to pull upward exposing not four; but eight sets of both long and short canine teeth, which together with the rest of the teeth made up a mouth of pristine white razors. The upper part of the head was conical, crowned like a macabre deep drum lampshade of sorts, with tufts of matted black hair spiked upward and slightly back. No ears were to be seen under all the black hair, but the outline of a face gave the impression of a cylinder of sorts. It wasn't a monkey, and it wasn't a gorilla. An "ape thing" is the only way to describe what was now glaring at Marina – even that description wouldn't be completely accurate.

It tilted its head, grimaced in disgust with its black canine lips and muttered what seemed to be unintelligible words in a chilling voice that ranged between nearly subsonic to falsetto. Then it turned its body and head to the right and left as if it had heard something and was checking to see that no one would disturb it as it carried out its dastardly deed. Marina noticed and even felt how its anger and hatred only grew toward her. Finally, it pointed to her with a black hairy claw and spoke in a churning, deep tone.

"Shuuu! Gruuuu!!!" it bellowed at the little girl from the other side of the glass.

Whatever it had said gave Marina the immediate impression that she was in deep, deep trouble. What had she done wrong? Why did this ape thing hate her – because she was human? She stood there frozen and obedient as if being disciplined by an adult.

All of this had not lasted more than a minute, but it seemed much longer to a little girl paralyzed by terror. A huge black arm immediately came crashing through the bedroom window. The shattering of all that glass should have alerted her mother and any neighbors to the danger. But for some reason it didn't. The flying pieces of glass had hardly settled on the floor, dresser and bed when the arm reached in and a claw picked Marina up by her hair. She screamed in pain, beating desperately with her little hands against the side and ribs of this monster, trying her utmost to alert her mother. Reportedly, her mother had heard absolutely nothing.

The monster had picked Marina up and tucked her firmly under its huge right arm, but with her feet facing toward the monster's path and unknown destination. It turned and began to walk with her toward the end of the backyard which faced the backyard of her own home at the foot of the embankment behind the fence. Marina saw the thousands of pieces of glass from the shattered window behind her do something incredible.

Within two seconds all of the pieces moved in exactly the opposite direction that they had only two minutes earlier, coming neatly together from the floor inside and the dresser and bed to seal the window which now looked as if it had never been broken. How would her mother even know to look for her? she wondered as the window and her grandparents' home quickly became smaller and smaller behind her.

Marina had always wondered what it would be like to fly. Now she was being whisked away from the house where her mother was at a speed she had never known was possible. The ape thing was so large and moved so fast and gracefully that in what seemed about three or four steps they had already gone over or perhaps even through the backyard fence. Now, moving quickly through the side yard of her own home and past the clothes lines supported by metal poles shaped like a "T", Marina began to scream as loud as she could. The monster stopped abruptly and dropped her to the ground.

In a few seconds they had come all the way from her grandparents' home on Ballistic over the fence and down the embankment to the end of her parents' house near Liberia. The monster tugged her hair twice so that a good sized tuft came loose. It was excruciating, and she cried. Then it leaned forward and furiously rebuked her in some unknown language.

"Gupallagullah! Gupallagullah!!!" it screamed with an almost falsetto voice right in her face, like an angry parent scolding a child.

She looked with her teary brown eyes into the horrific and evil glare, petrified with fear. This was *not* a parent trying to protect a child. This monster hated her! She could now smell the exotic, musk odor of the thing that had been carrying her. It was like the smell of the oil cloths her grandfather kept in his garage. Her instinct was that shared by many children − something so big and with such a strong, musk odor is to be obeyed and not to be trifled with.

The last fourth of a blazing red sun was quickly setting in front of them to the west as the monster again picked Marina up and locked her under its armpit to continue their deadly journey. Perhaps it was taking her westward to the Gulch − a desolate and wild area at the foot of the tablelands and just west of Harper and south of Daughn. There was little chance anyone would ever find her there alive.

The ape thing resumed their journey and proceeded to cross Liberia Avenue just as a blue and white Oldsmobile Fiesta station wagon screeched to a halt beside them, and the driver immediately threw the wagon into reverse, stripping the transmission. But then the young male driver noticed that the horrendous creature straining to see him through the headlights had a little human girl pressed between its arm and body. Despite disbelief at what he was witnessing, his fatherly instinct kicked in and he stopped the car, opened his door and started shouting and honking his horn.

Either the monster was angered by this or distracted by the headlights and horn. It dropped Marina to the asphalt with a thud, briefly covered its eyes with its black hairy claws, then turned and pushed the station wagon backward effortlessly with its hairy foot.

At first, Marina stood up but hesitated to run away. She was now nearly resigned to her fate and didn't want to disobey the monster and anger it more. But a brief memory of how the day had begun with her grandparents and mother flashed in her mind, awakening her from the deep trance she was in. That flash of reality was all that was needed for her to start running away from the heroic driver who was calling for her to get in and from the monster as it again gave the wagon a slight kick that nearly flipped it on its side.

38

Marina continued running around the corner from Liberia Avenue and slowed down to a walk on 14th Street as she passed the front yard of her own house on the right. There were no lights on. Nobody was home.

She heard the monster give out a horrible yell as the street lights automatically switched on and finally the thing retreated with an aggressive snort at the driver before it ran off – perhaps westward beyond the few houses which overlooked the Gulch. The driver pushed the gas pedal to the floor and sped off leaving only the sound of crickets and of dogs barking throughout the neighborhood.

In front of little Marina a glowing and dark yellow Westinghouse gumball streetlight came into view. That familiar street lamp, some distance away, marked the place of her salvation and safety, the only place or destination that existed now in her little mind.

With a torn and soiled dress and only one shoe on, little Marina walked forward in a daze toward the corner of Ballistic Avenue and 14th Street. There, she knew she would find a pink house, with the porch light on and a slanting, asphalt driveway that led to the front door. The monster that had nearly taken her life could have returned to claim her in this near total darkness only broken by the occasional streetlight. But it didn't.

Only a few moments after she noticed the porch light of her grandparents' home to her right, another car stopped in front of her on the side of 14th Street. She squinted and raised her arms in front of her eyes, blinded by the headlights. Luckily the driver had seen the little girl who could easily have been plowed down by oncoming cars as she walked slowly and serenely near the middle of the street. The driver was Marina's grandfather.

Grandpa and Grandma Ahnus showed up at the front door and rang the doorbell instead of directly letting themselves in. When Marina's mother opened the door and saw Grandfather holding Marina in his arms she glanced at them all, silent and expressionless, through the screen door for a few seconds. Grandpa's eyes blazed as he looked his daughter straight in the eyes. What kind of a mother are you? his expression depicted with clarity.

"Charles, set her down on the couch inside," Grandmother said to Grandfather, as if trying to break some magic spell that kept Grandfather's and Marina's mother's eyes fixed on each other.

Grandpa Ahnus obliged his wife, pulled back the screen door with his foot, went in and laid Marina to rest on the living room couch. Now they all noticed Marina's torn dress, the missing shoe and the fact that she was completely silent now and sucking her thumb like an infant. Shock set in as Marina's mother finally grasped that something incredible and horrible had occurred that she knew absolutely nothing about. Her daughter was at least for now incapable of letting them know what had happened to her.

And then the screaming in Estonian began with, "Kuidas sa tüdruk nii kohutavalt küündimatu ema oled, kuna sa oma lapsi ei suuda silmas pidada?!"

That roof-lifting diatribe, which roughly means "Daughter, how can you be such a lousy mother that you can't even keep an eye on your child?!", came from Marina's grandfather who was now basically hysterical. Nobody dared answer.

And soon they were all hysterical and wondered if they should take Marina to Newland Beach Memorial Hospital. After checking her over for signs of cuts or broken bones and finding only a few minor bruises and scrapes, they decided to wait until morning. No one even knew what they would say to a doctor about what had happened to Marina.

No one slept that night – especially not Marina. She didn't dare sleep. Just on the back of her eyelids, whenever she would shut them for more than a short moment, was the face of the monster that had kidnapped and nearly killed her – the thing that hated her. She lay next to her mother in the front bedroom of her grandparents' house slowly recalling what had happened to her.

After some hours and when the sun began to come up she remembered very well everything that had happened. She remembered those eyes. And then she began to scream.

ॐ ॐ ॐ

My sister Marina swears that this event happened. She has never changed a word, added a detail or even looked away when she has spoken about it. Our father was away on a business trip that week. But when he returned he recorded my sister's account with his real-to-real tape recorder, and we still have that tape. Our grandfather drove round the neighborhood and even stopped to talk to neighbors who lived near the intersection where the ape thing had dropped Marina and confronted the young driver who probably saved her life.

The only suspicious activity neighbors remembered was a strange blue and white Oldsmobile Fiesta wagon they had never seen before. The car had slowly driven around the neighborhood that evening, as if the driver was looking for someone. Since Marina had mentioned a male driver who had confronted the ape thing, everyone began to wonder if he was in reality a pervert responsible for her attempted abduction.

My grandfather began to believe this version and swore he would put a bullet in the man with his elephant gun if he ever laid eyes on him. Nobody has seen that driver or his car since that horrible evening.

No one can explain how Marina got over her grandparents' fence and ended up out on Liberia Avenue. She could hardly reach the bedroom light switch. Still, they theorize that she managed to climb the fence, tear her dress and hop down the embankment to her own backyard below, perhaps losing a shoe on the way. As for the damaged section of fence where the thick creosote wood post now leans almost ten degrees, neighbors and family say there could be all kinds of plausible explanations.

Neither Grandpa Ahnus nor Marina's father could explain the impressions in both their backyards which were very reminiscent of huge, heavy footprints. Instead of explaining, they leveled out the impressions with new dirt and tried to forget.

Priit and Esther Tamm became very anxious when they heard that a monster had broken in and kidnapped little Marina only yards from their own house. Mr. Tamm installed floodlights in his side- and backyard within a week of hearing Trisha's rendition of Marina's story.

Mrs. Tamm comforted Marina and cried when she heard the whole ordeal directly from Marina about a year later. A few weeks after that, Trisha came over with a new dress Mrs. Tamm – an excellent seamstress – had made just for Marina.

Marina never played or slept in that room again. Virginia Ahnus, her grandmother, took over the back bedroom and used it as her meditation room. There, Grandmother would often lay – propped up steeply by too many pillows – upon the four-poster bed, listening in tears to classical music. Other times she just lay quietly repeating Spanish phrases incorrectly to herself as she tried for years – unsuccessfully – to follow a five-LP Spanish course she had bought at a garage sale.

4

THE TAMMS: SOVIET ESTONIA WOULD HAVE BEEN A BETTER FATE
1972

The Tamm family came to the United States in 1952 when the Patriot Palaces homes on the west side of Harper were being erected over the covered military airfield and barracks nobody wanted to remember. Both Priit and Esther Tamm were born Estonian citizens in the late 1920's. But since the 1940's Estonia was no more, save for a handful of older men who considered themselves — and were in fact considered by the United States and Canada — a sort of government, or at least diplomats in exile. Their job was to act as a liaison between the countries hosting the Estonian diaspora and refugees and those Estonians who wanted to keep in touch with something that could be considered a remnant of the independent republic they had known.

Technically, since many countries considered Estonia in practice part of the Soviet Union, including the Soviet Union itself, these Estonians were now citizens of the Union of Soviet Socialist Republics. They were also citizens of the recently-invented Estonian Soviet Socialist Republic which had its own government and ministers for various affairs. The KGB, which many are familiar with, was like the United States Central Intelligence Agency or CIA. GRU, the Main Intelligence Directorate of the USSR, which many have not heard of, was very actively involved in operations in foreign countries. Defectors and Cold War immigrants were of special interest to GRU. People like the Tamms had a strategic bullseye painted on their foreheads.

As citizens of the Soviet Union, the Tamms were only entitled to Soviet Passports if they wanted to travel. And applying for such passports would, in fact, have meant a one-way journey for the Tamms back to Soviet Estonia, where the passports would have been cancelled and new ones likely refused. Passports still sometimes issued by the exile Estonian consulate general were not normally considered real passports by countries other than the United States and Canada. But since they had arrived legally, the United States provided the Tamms with travel documents for non-citizens. Trisha, their daughter who had been born in Toronto, was a natural born Canadian citizen which meant that maybe Canada would let them stay if the United States ever expelled them for some reason.

Nobody trusted anyone in the new Soviet Estonia. Less than two years after Priit and Esther had fled the homeland, neighbors in their former town were dressed up in Soviet military police uniforms ordering people they had lived next to, eaten dinner with, worked with or gone to school with to pack their things and be ready for prison or labor camp transport in five minutes.

The postman who had delivered their mail when they were teenagers had reportedly joined the security forces with great Communist fervor and executed Esther's brother's entire family outside the family's house one February morning. They were, after all, *kulaks* – a family who owned ten or more acres of farmland.

One of Esther's and Priit's teachers had been arrested and deported to a labor camp near Magadan, because her colleague – another one of their former teachers and now a Communist party member – had reported her as an "antirevolutionary Estonian nationalist and a fascist" who had once belonged to the Estonian Women's' League. Priit's family house now occupied the illustrious role as the main office building of the local People's Executive Committee for their town.

God only knew what brutal and crazed lunatics were now marching through the halls and rooms of the house where Priit and even his parents had been born and played as children. Had these new and unwelcome occupants perhaps stumbled upon personal papers of Priit or his parents and family?

This information and more had come from others who had managed to flee via Sweden and Germany after the Tamm family had left. The Estonian consulate network in exile would share many of these alarming tidbits of information with those families who had registered or who otherwise were known to them. For this reason, the Tamms were very thankful to and actively in contact with the exile Estonian consulate in New York City and with various older members of the Estonian Committee – the so-called bowtie men.

Toward the end of the 1960's when GRU and the KGB were actively infiltrating peace movements, leftwing political parties and even emigrant organizations, the Tamms began to wonder what might happen to them if the Soviets managed to plant a mole in or infiltrate the Estonian Committee. Perhaps not *all* of the bowtie men were working for the cause of a liberated Estonia or the welfare of its citizens. Was it really such a good idea that information about the Tamms and their families back in Estonia was in the hands of any organization? they began to wonder.

Fearing that the Estonian Committee or even the consulate might be infiltrated or taken over by the Soviets, the Tamm family began to distance themselves even from these organizations which had provided a lifeline to their homeland and to other Estonians. And they began to prepare for the long process of applying for United States citizenship out of fear that they might be sent back to the Soviet version of their homeland if relations improved between the USSR and the United States. Now they had one more child – a son named Patrick – who was a natural born US citizen. He was born in 1962 at Newland Beach Memorial Hospital.

Patrick had a large head, freckles and the same short, strawberry blonde hair and grey eyes as his father to whom he was very close. He was not as close to Esther, his mother, or to his sister Trisha. At times it seemed as though they merely tolerated each other. He kept to himself, confiding almost solely in his father, often peering through his 30-inch telescope in the backyard at night or reading books about space and the solar system. His father Priit was everything to him, and he wanted to follow in Priit's footsteps and eventually take up work as a machinist at the cable factory over on the corner of Shrapnel and Shell Shock in Harper. However, Patrick's father thought that he should study at college and become an engineer – maybe even a rocket engineer. None of this was to be.

During the first half of 1972 the twenty America-years of the Tamm family constituted a literal middle-class success story of Cold War immigrants arriving in poverty, getting work, taking up loans and purchasing a single-story house in the quiet suburbia of Harper, California. Their daughter was already a Canadian citizen and their accents were becoming all the more subtle, prompting both Priit and Esther to sometimes tell a white lie that they were from Canada — Quebec, for instance. This of course, was only to total strangers, because you never knew if the seemingly friendly stranger striking up a conversation might be someone sent by the Soviet consulate or embassy to keep tabs on emigrants or "defectors" as the Soviet government referred to them.

1972 was also the year their daughter, Trisha, went off to Canada to college. Tuition was cheaper there, and Trisha began packing in March, moving away in the middle of April. Marina constantly hugged her best friend and they often cried. Both had now grown their hair down to their buttocks and could at times be seen with hippie-style flower crowns. Trisha's was particularly striking as she had jet black hair just like her mother was always said to have had at some time, seemingly unknown to anyone save Esther and her husband.

Those last few weeks Trisha and Marina would sit inside at the same corner table of the A&W Root beer Drive-thru diner on 13th Street, where inside dining tables were few and far between and customers in cars were still served by carhops in A&W uniforms on roller skates. Little had changed since the 1950's, when either the Tamms or the Ahnus's would make one obligatory visit a week with the two little girls who were inseparable. Now Harper, the yellow lathed plaster house she called home and all of these shared and special places would soon be little more than a memory for Trisha Tamm. She would now plot out her own life alone in a strange country whose passport she held and where she had been born – a country otherwise foreign to her.

"I can't believe you're going away!" Marina would whine while drawing out the last word for what seemed like a half minute.

"Honey, there are telephones and there are airplanes and there are college guys!" Trisha would cheerfully console her virtual younger sister Marina.

The seemingly repetitive ritual was always and without exception concluded with mutual giggling, crying and then a long, rocking hug.

The last words Trisha spoke to Marina before Trisha got on the morning plane to Toronto at Los Angeles International Airport were "Look out for your little brother and mine! There have been so many creepy things happening lately in Harper! Love you!"

⋄   ⋄   ⋄

For Patrick Tamm, who turned ten in May, 1972 was the summer when he in practice became an only child. Family negotiations were underway for Patrick to immediately inherit Trisha's room – the spacy side bedroom nearest the driveway and the Ahnus's house next door. Patrick didn't care if Trisha thought she had been observed many nights by a black figure wearing a fedora hat and standing at the foot of her bed.

He would often half-joking say to his father in Estonian "Noh Isi, kui meie majas elab keegi teine, nii ma hakkan temalt üüri nõudma!" and his father would always laugh. In English, it meant that if somebody or something else was living in their house, he would start demanding that it pay rent.

June came with overcast mornings and unusually warm sunny afternoons adorned with pure blue skies. White butterflies, brushfoots and skippers – which Grandma Ahnus who was from Kentucky called "millers" – would visit one carnation and continue to another and then move on in the Ahnus' backyard to the red geraniums that Grandma Ahnus watered nearly every afternoon. These flowers along with myriads of others were scattered around the edges of the backyard in flowerbeds near the back part of the pink one-story house or near the patio and creosote wood fence which marked the boundary of Grandpa's and Grandma's backyard.

Patrick Tamm would occasionally climb up on the first side rail which supported the Tamm's side of the creosote wood fence and spy over the course, splintery pickets into the neighboring backyard – sometimes even when I was hunting for butterflies and spiders. But those times had ended more than a year ago and save for Grandma Ahnus' visits to water the flowers and pick weeds, the grassy backyard was now almost always empty of people. The Tamm's backyard had steadily since the mid 1960's become one giant cemented driveway and patio between their side yard and the detached garage at the back of their property. Their yellow house and garage had few vestiges of nature and Mrs. Tamm – a very busy seamstress – would not have had time to keep up a garden anyway.

One unusually sunny morning during the first week of June 1972 Patrick had left the house via the back door from his sister's old bedroom and stood in his backyard near the garage straightening his backpack. As he started to walk down the driveway via the side yard, he noticed that someone was standing on the other side of the fence in the Ahnus' backyard.

"Kas seal on keegi?" (Anybody there?), he called in Estonian, assuming that it was Mr. or Mrs. Ahnus or one of their grandchildren. He was met by total silence.

Could it be a prowler or burglar? he began to wonder. In that case, he would scare the prowler off, he decided. Patrick put his thumb and index finger against his mouth and whistled loudly as he walked toward where he had seen the suspected prowler. Again, there was nothing but silence. The pointed picket fence was nearly six feet high and the spacing between the thick, splintery boards was less than a quarter of an inch. It was almost impossible to successfully make out any features on the other side. Still, he could make out the shadow of a person, most likely an adult, just on the other side. The person was standing completely still now.

"What are you doing in their backyard, mister?" he asked, taking care not to mention whose backyard the possible intruder was in.

Still, not a word came from the motionless figure behind the fence. Patrick moved in closer to the fence – so close, in fact, that he could now smell the creosote from the course, splintery boards.

"What are you doing in their backyard, mister?" said an unexpected voice from behind the fence.

Patrick strained to keep from wetting his new blue jeans as he realized that the voice was an exact copy of his own, including his way of speaking. He was being mimicked perfectly by somebody or something the size of an adult.

"Kas seal on keegi?" the shadow behind the fence then mimicked with perfect Estonian pronunciation.

Now, the dark figure was imitating the voice of his father asking the question Patrick had asked barely two minutes earlier. Patrick could hear his own heart starting to pound in the middle of the silence as he backed away from the fence in horror.

As Patrick carefully stepped toward the side yard and driveway, the shadowy figure behind the boards did exactly the same. Then came a section in the fence where the boards weren't as close together. Now a dark figure, perhaps wearing a hat, became apparent to him. His fear only grew as the future engineer realized that this wasn't a person. Patrick's normally logical, inquisitive and courageous mind now drew a blank. He just wanted to get away. Then, he walked quickly down the driveway toward the open entry to the street- Ballistic Avenue.

His adversary on the other side of the fence also walked along the Ahnus' side yard and past their clothes lines toward the entry to the street, exactly across from Patrick. If Patrick now reached the street, they would come face to face and stare each other right in the eyes. Patrick, by basic instinct, now wanted to avoid such a fate at any price. He now moved quickly back toward the backyard and garage along the driveway – so did his unwelcome and sinister "shadow".

"Go away!" he yelled so that his voice echoed against the two houses.

The terror in his broken voice was quite apparent now. His instinct told him that whatever was on the other side of that fence was now enjoying itself. As he backed off planning to run to the kitchen window and beat on it to get his mother to open the back bedroom door which was now locked from the inside, the dark, shadowy figure on the other side began to rise up as though it were going to climb over the fence and toward Patrick. Now he could see a black fedora hat just above the pickets of the fence. He didn't want to see more.

Looking at the only clearly visible part of this creature – the hat – he noticed that it wasn't completely visible or stable like a regular physical object. The hat appeared slightly translucent and gave the impression that it was spinning at about 130 rotations per minute. What kind of being is this? he wondered in an almost scientific way briefly forgetting that he himself was now the hunted and not the observer.

Patrick Tamm then tried a little experiment. He took three steps forward toward the very thing that was now causing him to wet his pants. Indeed, his move now brought a temporary victory and a slight relief as the shadowy figure now backed down and was again completely behind the fence. This was clearly a ghoulish game of chess.

56

Whatever this thing was, it was intelligent and it was toying with him.

Since the figure on the other side of the fence was partially translucent, perhaps it wasn't completely solid and wouldn't be able to physically harm him. This was Patrick's reasoning, as he looked toward the driveway and the street. He would make a run for it. But apparently this thing that was now trying to scare Patrick to death could also read his thoughts. He heard a loud thump on the ground in the Ahnus' yard behind the fence. It must have been a foot or boot being resolutely stamped.

Not three seconds had gone by when a deafening bang almost like an explosion echoed between the houses as something clobbered the old creosote wood fence. The entire length of the fence rocked – even the support posts. The dust that had once covered the fence was thrown off and blew away in the slight breeze. Patrick had jumped about two feet in the air and fallen to the ground. This was a very clear message regarding Patrick's hypothesis.

He rose up and got back on his feet, brushing the dust off but keeping a constant eye on the thing behind the fence. He didn't know what to do and his mother didn't seem to hear the horrible bang that had rocked the fence. Like a lighting strike out of nowhere Patrick saw a shadowy arm and then a torso bolt right through the fence. That's all he could remember seeing before there came a sickening blow to his chest that picked him up off the ground and sent him flying ten yards through the air into the splintery fence at the opposite side of the Tamms' yard. Esther Tamm did see him land.

આ ✅ ✅

One fiery red afternoon close to evening I was standing in my grandparent's backyard. The view too was striking and fiery red with what Grandma Ahnus told me was a buttermilk sky. That's why I dared to venture out into the backyard after the things that had happened at preschool and in the backyard some years earlier. As long as Grandma was there or nearby, I felt I would be fine. When Grandma went inside I decided to be brave and stay outside for a short while longer. I missed that backyard which had been a magical paradise of sorts for so many years — before I became afraid to be there.

We didn't see much of the Tamms since Patrick had ended up at Newland Beach Memorial Hospital with a concussion some weeks earlier. They didn't seem to want to talk about how he had fallen and ended up in the hospital. It had happened one morning when I was at school during the first week of June that year.

Maybe he had fallen off this bike? I had wondered. I had later heard he was much better and now finally saw him in their backyard getting his telescope ready to look at both the Moon and the planet Venus which were to be in near conjunction this night. Peering over the fence into the Tamm's backyard just like Patrick would do into our yard, I asked him if I could come over later and look through the telescope.

"I suppose," he said "but we'll have to get permission from Clay"

"Who's Clay?" I asked bewildered.

Patrick didn't answer and just kept adjusting and peering through the lens of his telescope. I was seven and Patrick was ten. I assumed he was just ignoring an irritating "squirt" who was three years younger than him. So I stepped back down from the fence and started to explore the magical backyard I had loved and missed so much.

It was indeed a fiery early evening as the last dark red rays of sunlight shown against the pink back wall of the lathed plaster house my grandparents lived in. But now the unexpected intrusion of an approaching woman with a basket full of laundry forced me to admit that as fiery as this fiery evening was, it was not as fiery as her reddish blonde hair. Nor was her reddish blonde hair in a swirly up-do as fiery as her infernal personality.

The intense-looking woman with round, ice blue eyes and about Trisha's age had approached from our side yard, apparently let herself in from the side yard gate

59

near the street. She had Patrick in tow, presumably to vouch for who she was.

"Out of the way, brat!" the freckled woman yelled and pushed me to the side and off the narrow cement sidewalk near the back of the house.

"That's Clay," Patrick muttered softly in an undertone full of resignation "better do what she says and not get on her nerves"

I turned and looked to find out where she had gone. She had walked into the semi-enclosed patio, opened the storage room door and yanked the string to the simple hanging lamp with the exposed light bulb just above my grandparents' clothes dryer. Now it was light inside the storage room and we came near to see what she was doing.

The brief glimpse I got of her gave the impression of a hot-tempered, mean-spirited and bossy woman with fanatical eyes. Why she was now with the Tamm family was a complete mystery to me, and Patrick hadn't said anything. I then asked him in Estonian, hoping this strange woman couldn't follow our conversation.

"It doesn't matter," Patrick muttered again just as resigned as before "She can understand Estonian, Russian, Spanish, German or any language".

"Sa oled tark jõmpsikas!" Clay said to Patrick, pulled the string to turn out the light and slammed the storage room door shut. That is Estonian for "you're a smart brat".

The quiet hum and clicking of the dryer could be heard behind the door.

"But my mom told me that Estonian is one of the hardest languages to learn," I said to Clay wondering how she could have learned the language my mother said was almost impossible for non-Estonians – including my father – to learn.

Clay walked resolutely back the same way she had come, checking to make sure that Patrick was still following close behind. The flip-flopping of her blue and white sandals grew fainter. She never answered my question.

"Clay said no," Patrick muttered lifelessly before disappearing around the corner of my grandparents' house.

It was now dark. But there would be no joint stargazing in the Tamm family's backyard this evening. I opened the back door and went back into the house and through the dark back bedroom, past the four-poster bed and toward the hallway which now smelled of Grandpa Ahnus' bean stew and garlic bread.

Dinner was ready. But I still kept wondering who Clay was and why Patrick and his family let her stay there and boss them around.

❧ ❧ ❧

The summer of 1972 was the summer that Grandpa and Grandma Ahnus took the potted rubber tree which had stood in the corner of the living room and planted it outside between the fence and the garage facing 14th street. I personally watched and assisted that late June day and was the first to water the newly-planted tree. Since my father was at sea filming a documentary and my mother worked nearly every day as a supervisor and accountant at the Two Guys department store in Daughn, I was allowed to live with my grandparents all summer.

Neither my grandparents nor I had seen much of the Tamms for nearly two weeks. When I told them about Clay they shrugged it off and just laughed about the unusual name which in English is usually the short form of Clayton.

"Maybe that's her last name?" my grandmother had posited.

"Well, it sure sounds queer for a girl!" my grandfather had opined.

Usually all three families in our little Estonian colony consisting of the Tamms, the Ahnus's and the Groffs would have our own joint celebration of the 4th of July. It had been a tradition since the 1960's. As the expected joint celebration approached, my grandmother received an unexpected telephone call from Esther Tamm. They would not be participating this year.

It was a brief call from a neighbor who was basically family to us and who usually visited personally and sat down for a cup of coffee when she had anything to report. Something was not right.

Grandpa had hardly seen the Tamms in their yard since the beginning of June. So he decided to go over and talk to Mr. Tamm in Estonian to see if everything was ok. Clay had opened the front door and let Priit Tamm – under her close observation – come to the door and talk to Grandpa Ahnus. Mr. Tamm made his best attempt to convincingly tell Grandpa that everything was fine and that they were just very busy right now.

But Grandpa immediately sensed that there was something off about Clay. In fact, he was even slightly afraid of her – something very unusual for Grandpa.

Now we were all worried, and my grandparents had me tell them everything that had happened the evening Clay had come over and used their dryer. I willingly obliged.

"Charles!" my grandmother then interjected "Maybe we could make copies of those Thanksgiving photographs and either go over or have Priit and Esther come over here!" she then proposed.

"We can try, but I don't think that strange woman will let them," Grandpa Ahnus replied while collecting the envelope with the negatives from his filing cabinet in the side bedroom. "We can take these over tomorrow when we drop the cleaning off at Mrs. Hanson's," he said as he laid back down on his side of the bed in the master bedroom.

"Charles," said Grandma in an alarmed voice "do you suppose she's one of those Charles Manson cult girls?"

"Well, she did have a fanatical look, but if she can understand all of these languages like Gordon says then she sounds more like–" Grandpa Ahnus stopped dead in the middle of his sentence. He now looked very worried. His eyes widened and he sat up on the bed. "Kuradi kõik!" he yelled in Estonian, meaning "damn it all".

Grandma, who had been sitting on her side of the bed with her back to Grandpa turned around with eyes as big as dish plates, wondering what had gotten into him. She now had the expression of an animal caught in headlights.

"Charles?" she asked "What's the matter?"

64

"Virginia," he answered, using her first name — something he rarely ever did — "that woman is probably a goddamn Soviet agent trying to take Priit, Esther and Patrick back to that goddamn Communist hellhole!"

Now both of them looked exceedingly worried.

I doubt my grandparents or I got much sleep that night. However, the oddest thing for me was the fact that I had this horrible sensation of sadness and longing for the Tamms. We were close families and neighbors, but this was an uncharacteristic emotion. I thought about Patrick walking away that evening some weeks ago. Was he ok? Was he sad? Was I ever going to see him again? I kept wondering to myself. And I started to cry.

When we dropped the cleaning off at Mrs. Hanson's on 13th Street the following day, Grandfather stayed inside talking to Mrs. Hanson for more than an hour. Clearly, from the gestures and expressions seen through the front glass window, both of them were up in arms about something. Grandma finally opened her door and then I did the same. We both got out of the brown Dodge four-door sedan which my sister Marina had dubbed "the Brown Clown", slammed our doors shut and proceeded to enter Mrs. Hanson's cleaning service.

Once inside, the door had hardly shut behind us and the hanging welcome bells were still ringing when Mrs. Hanson — roughly sixty years old — looked right at me with her big round blue eyes and a startling red faux bob hairstyle that could stop traffic and cried "Gordie Groff! Look how much this boy has grown!"

"This little boy has seen more than any kid his age should have to," she continued looking directly at Grandpa Ahnus.

My grandparents both nodded, looking at me and then back at Mrs. Hanson. They knew that she was aware of every strange occurrence in town.

The inside of Mrs. Hanson's dry cleaning shop was not much other than false wood paneling that was nearly invisible behind all of the rows of hanging blouses, coats, curtains and folded blankets – almost all draped in plastic with a paper tag stapled haphazardly somewhere. A little antique wooden desk stood between the entry and the various and sundry ironing and washing equipment. She didn't use a cash register. Everything was handled by scribbled notes and forms. The huge windows let in lots of light and I could see that Mrs. Hanson had on a simple gold summer dress with orange and blue flowers. This was her usual apparel from as early as any of us could remember.

My grandfather proceeded to fill his wife in with regard to what the discussion had been about. Things were taking a turn for the worse more hastily than my grandparents had imagined. Hardly a day prior, Clay herself had been to see Mrs. Hanson and drop off some cleaning for the Tamms. She had dropped off regular pants and shirts that Esther Tamm would have washed at home, according to Mrs. Hanson. And she had told Mrs. Hanson that the Tamms were going away on a very long trip.

"Esther does all of the normal wash at home," Mrs. Hanson repeated her suspicions to my grandmother. "She only brings in large carpets and her living room drapes, which she has cleaned once a year!" Mrs. Hanson concluded looking even more worried.

She paused thoughtfully, bit off a piece of one of her nails, spat it out and then looked right at my grandfather.

"If you ask me, I think the entire purpose of her visit was just to tell me basically not to suspect anything and that they were going away," she said with an expression that spoke of fear.

We left and dropped off the negatives at the QuickFoto booth. They gave my grandfather a receipt and told him to come back in a week. Grandpa and Grandma Ahnus knew — as if by instinct — that we didn't have that long.

At Helmet Center — a strip mall close to our home on 13th Street and like so many others in Harper and southern California — we visited Mrs. Hong's Supermarket. She had already formed an opinion of Clay and began walking toward my grandparents as soon as she caught sight of them entering the store.

"I don't like that lady!" was Mrs. Hong's first sentence-putting the emphasis on the last word when my grandfather asked whether she had seen anyone like Clay at the market. "She come here, tell me Mrs. Tamm and Mr. Tamm, whole family go away for a long time," Mrs. Hong said shaking her head.

We did our shopping and then went to the checkout where Mrs. Hong was sitting, looking at us very worried.

"Something very wrong!" the 40-year-old Korean store owner urged my grandparents.

Then she just shook her head again and rang up our groceries purchase on the cash register. Grandpa and Grandma Ahnus kept looking at each other in horror and disbelief intermittently as Mrs. Hong packed the groceries into brown paper bags.

From the supermarket we drove straight and without any delay to the police station on Mercy Shot Boulevard, where my grandfather spoke to an officer for an hour. Butter, ice cream and frozen vegetables from the supermarket melted in the paper grocery bags beside me on the back seat of the car as we anxiously waited.

Grandpa finally stormed out of the police station toward the car cursing wildly in at least Estonian and English.

"Those goddam bastards aren't going to do anything!" he screamed almost breathlessly at Grandma before he had even shut the car door. His thick-rimmed glasses were crooked and started to fall off until he took them off and whisked his hand through his thin blonde comb-over that had been lifted up by the wind.

"Those sons of bitches want Priit and Esther themselves to report that horrible woman!" he continued his outburst as he put his glasses back on and started the car. The motor roared and black fumes rose from the back of the old Dodge. Soon we were on our way back home with a fury.

I was only seven. But I must have aged several years from fear as Grandpa cursed and nearly drove into the utility pole with the gumball street lamp on the corner of 14th Street and Ballistic Avenue where they lived. The execration continued as they both grabbed grocery bags and we all went into the house.

Then, I took off out the front door again and toward the street down the driveway to see if Patrick or anyone was in the Tamms' front yard. It was empty and quiet as never before.

"Gordon!" my grandmother's voice screamed from behind the screen door "Don't go near that house!"

        ٫   ٬   ٭

Sometime during the night on the 28th of June I was awakened by the rattling of all the windows throughout my grandparents' house. I was sleeping in the side bedroom next to the back bedroom and directly across from the master bedroom where my grandparents were sleeping. Even my bed was shaking. A picture of my sister as a 3-year-old which hung on the bedroom wall in front of the bed came crashing to the uncarpeted floor. The frame and glass had obviously been broken.

Even the doors to the house were shaking as the temblor increased in intensity and was followed by thundering and groaning that I shall not forget as long as I live. It was as if a horrific howl had begun to emanate from the earth below. I immediately hopped up from the bed to look out the bedroom window which faced the Tamm family's home. The windows which were usually completely dark at this hour were lit up by what looked like flames. The red and yellow shimmering continued for a minute or so until I could adjust me eyes to investigate details behind the windows.

Through the side window of what was formerly Trisha's and had for barely a month been Patrick's bedroom, I saw no indication that Patrick was in the room or awake.

A huge plume of smoke and dust welled up from the other side of their house and there was a thunderous roar. Suddenly there was a silence intermittently broken by the sound of falling bricks and lumber. As I looked to the left I noticed that the door to my grandparent's kitchen flew open and Grandpa Ahnus bolted into the side yard trying to get a glimpse of what had happened. The lights outside then went out.

He was in his pajamas and so was I. I ran through the dark house to the kitchen, out the door and followed Grandpa as he opened the entry to the side yard. We both walked over the lawn in the dark toward the Tamm family's house.

"Charles! Gordon!" I could hear my grandmother calling from the kitchen doorway holding a flashlight. No sooner had we crossed the Tamm's lawn toward the entry when we noticed the blue flashes of light and electrical sparks coming from the part of the house which was still standing. It was the only light in the area which was now almost completely dark. Even the gumball street light at the corner of 14th Street and Ballistic Avenue was now dark, just like all other house and street lights for as far as I could see.

Had we had a major earthquake? I wondered. Neighbors were gathering in small groups with flashlights and moving carefully toward the Tamms' house. It was then I began to realize that whatever disaster had occurred, it was this particular house which had borne the brunt of it.

Others had beaten us to the area where there was no more sign of the Tamm family's home. As we all moved in slowly and carefully I began to hear the reactions of those who were in front of us. "Oh my God! Look at that!" echoed the voice of the first witness to see what had been left behind.

"Jesus! How deep is that?!" said another voice that had seen the deep hole.

No sign remained of anything that had fallen into the hole. Approximately one third of the Tamms' home had disappeared into it. The entire family was nowhere to be found in what remained. My grandfather and I pushed our way through the others to see what had happened to our friends, our family. There was not much left to see except for a very deep hole- so deep, in fact, that none of the flashlights could reach the bottom with their light. When we had had our glimpse, the sound of sirens began to grow louder until finally we were all ushered away from the site.

My grandfather counted ten fire, ambulance, police and other government cars, including the several that were now using his driveway. The only light we could see was that of the reddish overcast sky, lit up by those city lights which were still working somewhere.

Then the helicopters began to arrive.

Grandfather sat in his pajamas on the ledge of the concrete brick flowerbed near the front porch to his house. He was completely silent, rocking back and forth. When I saw him like that I became scared for the first time. Grandma came wearing her nightgown and put her frail arms around him for a while, and then we all went inside.

My grandparents' house and all properties bordering directly on the Tamms' lot were evacuated that very day, for fear that the ground might not be stable. For two months the city and the government examined the hole and wreckage eventually capping the site with a steel-reinforced seal more than four feet thick. Some workers had seen smoke coming from the hole. Others reported hearing eerie metallic and groaning sounds coming from the bottom of the hole for up to two days after the disaster. They estimated the depth to at least 1 380 feet, maybe more.

Trisha Tamm had made an appointment for the 29th of June with the Harper police and with a field officer from the FBI regarding the situation of her parents. Her mother had sent her letters which caused her to panic. And her parents wouldn't answer the telephone when she called. So she booked a plane home from Toronto. That plane landed in Los Angeles the morning of the disaster.

When Trisha met my grandparents who were staying with Aunt Jessica on Oaf Street, she was in shock and shared the contents of the letters with my grandfather. Grandpa Ahnus was never the same after that and began to drink quite heavily. Trisha was eventually admitted to a psychiatric hospital in Toronto and dropped out of college in Canada. Neither my sister, nor my grandparents every saw her after that fateful summer.

In August of 1972, we were able to return to my grandparents' house. The first day we arrived, I visited the backyard without delay. Standing there like a senile, lone soldier at attention on the backyard lawn that overcast, dewy morning was Patrick's telescope. Who had placed it there? I wondered. It then became clear that a little red envelope was taped to the accessory tray of the telescope tripod. There was a card inside. Both had become soggy and the writing was slightly smudged. My grandfather examined the writing which he clearly found unsettling and then read it to me with a dry mouth and a face that was as white as a sheet:

I know this hurts, kiddo. But you'll understand everything when you get older. Enjoy the telescope.
Love,
Clay

Grandpa Ahnus passed on the note and envelope to the FBI field agent in Los Angeles who was now investigating the disappearance of the Tamm family.

5

PIECES:
DEADLY ANIMATE,
INANIMATE MATERIAL
1970

When I was in preschool, my mother or my sister used to drop me off at 12th Street Preschool and Kindergarten early in the morning. My mother was on her way to work and my sister was on her way to college. They both listened to the same music which would blurt from the car as they took my hand and led me to the preschool gate. As songs like the Jackson 5's "I'll be There" would drone in the background Leida, my mother, or Marina, my sister, would push up the clasp of the steel chain-link fence, open the gate and lead me to the entrance where Mrs. Junney or Mrs. Morel would take my hand and lead me inside.

I don't have any memories of separation anxiety or crying when they dropped me off. Mrs. Junney and Mrs. Morel liked me and I knew it. And I liked the other children. I felt safe at my little preschool on the corner of 12th Street and Liberia Avenue. The main front yard of the preschool was full of wonderful sandy and grassy places to play and explore. The backyard and side yard were amply equipped with tractor tires, slides, jungle gyms and even chickens or ducks, from time to time. Across from the front and side yards on 12th Street was a red and white country house with a small wooden fence. An older girl dressed in flannel blouses and with braided pigtails would often play in that yard just across the street.

I remember dewy mornings that were colored in bright yellow and lime. As we played outside, trucks would sometimes drive by the schoolyard on Liberia Avenue filling the air with the scent of moist alfalfa. Our childish adventures were regularly interrupted as Mrs. Junney or Mrs. Morel would call us back inside for a snack. But before the snack, we were to wash our hands in large, recycled coffee cans full of soapy and non-soapy water, dry them and then go inside. After snacks we would draw or paint. Soon after, it was time for lunch which was served at long tables set in a row.

When we had eaten we could climb into our cots for the hour-long obligatory naps. Once awake again we would sit, groggy and half-asleep, in front of the television watching the afternoon children's shows, eating graham crackers. Then, one by one, we were collected by our parents, retrieving our things from our cubby holes right below the windows near the entrance. For those who had long to wait, a second round of play dough art was arranged.

April, Jazon, Choi and I were often picked up rather late by our parents. So to pass the time, I would lead our little group in play, insisting that we all hummed the melody and imitate the synthesizer from the Sunday Mystery Movie theme from "Columbo". April always obliged.

The memories of a five-year-old are certainly fragmentary at best. Perhaps even false memories are mixed in with the fragmentary real ones. My advice to anyone wanting to substantiate or disprove childhood memories of events is to examine the reactions and words of the adults involved in the incident.

I know that Mrs. Junney moved back to Europe in 1979. Mrs. Morel moved to another state in 1980 and eventually changed her name. She, like the parents of some of my preschool mates, was tired of being hounded by reporters and self-styled cryptozoologists looking for decades-old information.

The newspapers of the time only state that there was an accident at 12th Street Preschool and Kindergarten. No reporters actually made it to the preschool before ambulances and city health officials had left. There are no pictures in the newspapers of officials with breathing masks and protective suits carrying away tens of glass jars, occasionally gazing in disbelief at the contents.

There is one picture of a pool of blood on the sidewalk leading to the entrance gate. I'm pretty sure whose blood it was, because I was there when it all happened. In fact, I still dream about that day about four or five times a year. My psychiatrist always told me that it might take years or decades, but that the nightmares would eventually decrease in number. He told me to try to face my fear, but gave me tranquilizers and sleeping pills just in case that didn't work. I don't think he really believed or wanted to believe my description of events. He had read the copies of the newspaper reports which I gave him.

Dr. Woodward often asserted that I must have embellished my memories of the events of September 19th, 1970 with a good-sized smattering of childhood imagination. However, if I follow my own advice from just a few paragraphs ago a problem arises. If Dr. Woodward is correct then Jazon choked on some inanimate foreign object he was playing with in the front yard of our preschool. Maybe the object was very sharp. That could explain the profuse bleeding.

Mrs. Junney's hysterical screaming and hesitation to help him when she saw that April and Choi were also struggling for their lives could have been some form of emotional overload or hysteria. But why was she pulling children away from the entire yard into the preschool building instead of helping Jazon, April and Choi? Why was she shutting all of the windows? Why was she examining the mouths, hands and clothes of children who were not even near the unfortunate 5-year-old victims before she would let them inside? And why was Mrs. Morel, who came running from the back of the preschool after hearing the turmoil, suddenly just as apprehensive as Mrs. Junney, refusing to go near the three suffering preschoolers?

Mrs. Junney was a 55-year-old stalky woman with blonde hair in a beehive whose hands spoke of hard labor and endurance. She had lived through the Second World War in Europe. Unless you believe that she would run from butterflies and evacuate an entire schoolyard for the sake of such a personal phobia, then Mrs. Junney's actions indicate that the danger was very real.

Mrs. Morel's brunette bouffant hairstyle couldn't conceal a pair of green eyes that clearly had seen just about everything in her sixty years of life. She was composed, even somewhat cynical and equally resourceful – not the type to panic. If she had ascertained that there was a serious danger, she would have quickly hatched a plan to bring everyone to safety. In part, she did. It was Mrs. Morel who contacted the authorities and warned frantic parents to wait an hour before picking up their children.

At least three families know the real story behind the 12th Street Preschool incident of 1970. They know, because they were asked to identify their dead and mutilated children. These families also know that the chance of all three preschoolers having died from choking, severe brain damage and hemorrhaging caused by inanimate pieces of material is remote. They had to bury their children in sealed coffins without saying a last goodbye, because they were told by health officials that there was a biohazard risk.

All of this started on a beautiful autumn day when I was playing in my grandparents' backyard. Butterflies and insects of all kinds were still to be found, and I was hunting for them with my newly-acquired insect catcher kit from the dime store over on Crocker Street on the east side of town. I was getting bored with the common white butterflies that were always in abundance in the garden. The real excitement came when something totally new and unknown came flying or crawling along.

That Saturday morning, I didn't have long to wait before something really exotic made its way to the little sidewalk near the semi-enclosed patio. As I stood on the lawn of the backyard scanning the area for whatever was flying around, I noticed something black fluttering about and then landing on the sunny concrete sidewalk. Now I had found myself something very unusual! As I slowly and carefully approached so as not to frighten the presumed butterfly away, my disappointment started to grow.

Clearly, this was not a butterfly or any insect at all. It was just a piece of chipped paint or perhaps a small bit of plastic. The little piece of unknown material was irregular in form as you would expect with chipped paint or a broken off piece of thin plastic. It was about an inch in diameter and as thin as a piece of paper. There was just one significant anomaly – this piece of "paint" or "plastic" was rolling and scurrying around on its own, apparently without the help of the breeze.

Then, before I knew what to think, another one landed right next to it. This one was a silvery color, like a piece of electrical tape. As if trying to make some kind of diversity statement, still a third specimen of these seemingly impossible creatures landed close to the other two. The new arrival was red in color. As a five-year-old I didn't fully appreciate how fantastic this situation was. An adult would surely have been trying to figure out how the creatures were able to move, see, fly and eat. Which end was the head? I did manage to wonder.

The silver creature then flew off so quickly that I could barely keep track of where it went. When I again caught sight of it, it was fluttering like a moth or butterfly near the backyard fence. I looked down at the red and black ones which were just sitting there completely still. Resourceful, as young children tend to be when it comes to finding names for hitherto unknown phenomena, I appropriately dubbed the new and anomalous creatures "pieces".

Having grown tired of the lack of movement of the two pieces in front of me, I looked around and grabbed a twig from the lawn. Once I started poking the black piece, it began to pulsate and curl itself up in some type of defensive posturing. Grandpa and Grandma had taught me to be careful with bees, wasps and spiders as they could sting or bite. I had no idea what these new creatures might be able to do.

I would soon find out for myself why I should have left well enough alone and quickly gone back into the house. But I decided I was curious as to whether the red piece was hard or soft. I had hardly placed my index finger on it to find out, when I felt a slight stinging sensation. One of the edges of the red piece had curled in toward my finger and penetrated the skin much like a small splinter of wood.

Lifting my finger, I noticed that the red piece was attached to it by the edge that had penetrated the skin. It didn't really hurt that much, and there was no blood. I made my second mistake of trying to touch the red piece and pull it from my finger. Immediately upon touching it, I found out that it was merely attached to my finger in order to anchor itself for something else.

The unattached opposite end of the piece bent as far as it could away from the skin of my finger. Then I felt and heard a snap, as though my finger had been struck with a rubber band. The stinging pain grew as I realized that this extremely strong and quick little predator had

82

pounced with the free edge and penetrated the skin of my index finger all the way to the bone. The blood began to drip from the wound where the attacking end of the red piece was still buried. I instinctively tried to remove the red piece with the thumb and index fingers of my other hand. When I touched the feisty thing it immediately removed the end it had used to anchor itself before the attack and attached that end to the thumb of the hand I was using to remove it.

Another snap revealed to me the situation I was now in and how incredibly fast and strong this horrible creature was. Now I had one index finger and one thumb with gashes to the bone dripping with blood. There was enough blood on the sidewalk now to attract the attention of the black piece which had been completely still during the complete ordeal. It rolled itself toward the little puddle of blood, then straightened itself out and appeared to reach toward it with one edge, as if possibly drinking from it in some unknown way.

It is impossible to say if these creatures were in some way attracted to the scent I gave off as I panicked or if they somehow keyed in on the carbon dioxide of my breath. Both the red piece that had attacked me and the black piece flew into the air, hovered near my face and then landed on my shirt. Now I perceived them to be making a very slight chirping sound almost like birds. The silver piece returned now and landed close to the others on my shirt. They were swarming.

I rolled up the brown and yellow Hang Ten shirt over my stomach and chest as fast as I was capable and pulled it over my head throwing it as far away as I could before running to the back door. Tearing at the knob with blood-covered hands that slipped, I finally got it open and ran inside. My grandparents were hysterical and completely confused when they caught sight of me.

When I told Grandpa Ahnus what had happened he went outside. The next I saw of him he was burning the abandoned shirt in the grill in the backyard. The iodine Grandma Ahnus put on both wounds hurt more than the original fiendish attack, which neither my mother nor my father could believe. For more than two years I had a phobia of the very backyard I had loved so much.

∽ ∾ ∾

Mrs. Morel was wearing a simple brown sheath dress that morning and stood together with Mrs. Junney in the main room of the preschool. It was the 19th of September, a reddish morning so typical of that time of year in Harper. Both preschool teachers were watching and instructing as we preschoolers marched in a circle to the music of "March of the Wooden Soldiers" which was blurting from the wooden extension loudspeaker mounted near the ceiling. We were finally released from our morning music appreciation exercise and everyone flooded into the front yard to play.

The swings were already taken, as often was the case, by the younger preschoolers. So April, Choi, Jazon and I were forced to find something interesting to do near the huge tractor tire which also served as a sandbox. It is difficult to remember exactly what activity we finally settled on. However, it must have been very short-lived, since Jazon and the rest of us caught sight of a silvery object which had attached itself to the side of the tractor tire. I immediately recognized what it was. None of the other kids did.

With neck-long blonde hair like string beans bouncing about, Jazon got up and ran round to the other side of the tractor tire and started looking for a twig or stick. He too was curious about these creatures. I pulled April's hand back as she moved it toward the silver piece on the tire. April looked at me crossly and pulled her arm away from me as though she would soon try to hit me. She didn't understand why I had intervened. I also mulled Choi's attempt to touch the strange organism. This time I got popped on the side of the head by the red-haired Choi who was notoriously bellicose. He raised his fist again threatening to repeat the defiant gesture if I tried to stop him from touching the object of his curiosity.

Jazon returned with a good-sized stick just before we were literally saved by the bell. The piece that he had planned to molest with the stick was much larger than the ones I had seen in Grandpa and Grandma Ahnus' backyard.

It was surely at least five inches or more in diameter. It had seemed rather docile and immobile, outright boring in comparison with the pieces that had attacked me earlier. We heard footsteps quickly approaching.

"Listen you children, it's time to come in and drink our juice now," Mrs. Junney scolded us in a thick German accent. She stood over us in her green, yellow and white floral sheath dress quickly polishing the lenses of her yellow horn-rimmed glasses with a napkin. Upon re-donning her glasses she promptly gave a stern look through the lenses at us and we ran inside.

For the better part of that morning we drank our grape juice in paper cups, sang and finger-painted. I don't know whether I contemplated our return to the play-yard with apprehension or if I perhaps was thinking about informing Mrs. Junney about the potential danger outside. I simply can't remember. April, Choi and Jazon were certainly excited and had every intention of returning to the tractor tire to examine the unusual specimen.

When we were again ushered outside for our pre-lunch playtime in the yard Jazon shot off directly in the direction of the black tire. April and Choi naturally followed suit. I trailed slowly behind them. There was a slight breeze and I could smell the freshly cut grass. The sky was a deep blue without a single cloud. All over the yard children were skipping, running, sitting, swinging, screaming and playing. Mrs. Junney was making lunch.

April was kneeling near Jazon with a brown twig, and her little yellow skirt was already covered with grass and sand when I showed up. Choi was staring blankly at the side of the tire where the organism had been when we all went inside. The large silver-colored piece which had simply rested, attached to the side of the tire was now not one; but six or seven separate pieces. It had apparently reproduced or divided itself into many individuals which were each curling their edges slightly back and forth while remaining attached by one edge to the tire.

Each of the new individuals was irregular in shape like a torn-off piece of plastic or electrical tape. They looked like pieces of inanimate material breaking the laws of nature and moving like living organisms. We were all fascinated, mesmerized by something we had never seen before. Then the inevitable childhood interest in poking and picking got the best of Jazon and April.

Both April and Jazon began poking the pieces with their twigs and the pieces would move away from the twigs by doing a bizarre somersault along the surface of the tire. One free edge would dig into the surface of the tire while the attached edge would then release itself from the tire. Then the free edge would curl in on itself in a defensive posturing which was familiar to me from the pieces in my grandparents' back yard.

Jazon moved in closer, probably wondering if these creatures had heads somewhere or eyes or small legs.

Several of the pieces then extended their free edges toward Jazon. He kept on examining them and poking around with his twig. Suddenly, faster than anyone's eyes could even follow, one of the pieces on the tire just disappeared into thin air − or so it seemed.

I heard a slight popping sound from Jazon's throat as he took a breath. Jazon's expression slowly became one of surprise and then confusion ultimately transforming into one of fear as he started to struggle to breath. No sooner had this all begun when another of the pieces on the tire shot quicker than a bullet from its resting place right into Jazon's mouth. April immediately ran to summon Mrs. Junney when she heard the horrible retching and coughing and saw Jazon sticking his hand in his mouth as his eyes watered profusely.

Choi, who had always been somewhat of an aggressive bully, was now whimpering as he watched Jazon fall to the ground and we all heard the slight whistling sound as he squirmed and fought desperately for even a slight breath of air. He kept reaching into his mouth as tears poured down his face and his eyes began to roll upward. As he tossed and turned intermittently clutching his throat in agony, blood began to stream from his mouth and nose. The repetitive, muffled snapping sound coming from his neck must have been the violent movements of the pieces he had in his trachea, burrowing into the tissue and cutting him to pieces from within.

I now heard the familiar faint chirping sound coming from the pieces which remained on the side of the tire. That this sound preceded aggression on the part of these infernal creations was only confirmed when two of the pieces from the tire shot toward Choi, one attaching itself to his face and the other to his blue and yellow knit sweater. Choi didn't have a chance to pluck off the piece on his face. Almost instantly, it had somersaulted along his skin upward to locate an apparently acceptable orifice into which it could burrow. And it did.

Choi quickly lost all interest in the danger located on the front of his knit sweater as he screamed at the top of his lungs in agony. He fingered his right eye and ran frantically and blindly until the piece on his sweater sensed the carbon dioxide coming from his screaming mouth and flew right in. Now Choi began to cough and retch just as Jazon had only minutes earlier. And soon Choi too was laying on the grass clutching at his throat, ignoring the by now largely destroyed eye from which blood was literally squirting.

I ran to find Mrs. Junney who was just coming out of the door with her apron still on from making lunch. Mrs. Junney began to scream as she first caught sight of Jazon who was now slightly convulsing in a rhythmic manner and apparently was no longer conscious. Choi was still continuing the by now all-too-familiar last struggle for breath. April who had come out together with her tried to show Mrs. Junney where the attackers had come from.

As Mrs. Junney began to examine Jazon's now lifeless body and then stumbled on to try to help Choi, April cried for her to come see what had caused the boys' debacle. Other preschoolers had now begun to assemble near the area of the incident. Younger children began to cry and older ones stood silent as if in a trance looking at the tire, the two bodies and a hysterical Mrs. Junney.

"Mrs. Junney! Mrs. Junney!!" April kept crying over and over again while pointing at the abandoned black tire where two or three pieces were still presumably in wait for more victims.

"April, dear," Mrs. Junney said as she got caught in her apron, stumbled briefly and then ripped the apron off "what did this? Was it a wasp or a bee?"

Mrs. Junney now ran quickly toward April, her yellow and white floral apron laying close to Choi who by now was as lifeless as Jazon. If Mrs. Junney really wanted an answer to the "what" and "how" of this schoolyard bloodbath, April would now involuntarily provide a demonstration. Mrs. Junney had scarcely reached April and the tire when two of the remaining pieces entered her nose and her eye.

Mrs. Junney had now seen the danger with her own eyes and was incredulous but terrified. The other kids began to scream as they also had seen what happened and how April was now digging at her nose and her eye and issuing a nearly constant high-pitched scream.

90

April by now already begun to choke on her own blood as the incessant, muffled snapping sound of the pieces could be heard from somewhere inside her nose and head. Mrs. Junney immediately understood that this was not a typical first-aid emergency. She had to get the other kids inside to safety.

Mrs. Morel had come running from the back preschool yard through the side yard and thrown open the gate between that yard and the front yard. Mrs. Junney tried to explain to her what she had seen when one of the pieces started to cut through Jazon's throat from inside, apparently having fully satisfied its appetite and wanting to leave. Mrs. Morel saw this upon examining Jazon's body and realized that nobody at the school was equipped to deal with this kind of danger.

A chirping sound could be heard as a partially bloody silver piece cut a slit through the trachea and skin of Jazon and flew off. Now three lifeless children's bodies littered the once-lovely preschool yard. Both preschool teachers started to bring children to safety inside and to make calls to paramedics to try to provide a cogent description of something hardly believable. Clothes, hands and mouths were systematically examined by Mrs. Junney before those in line could be admitted. Once inside, children were forbidden from going out again and Mrs. Junney shut and sealed all of the school windows and doors.

Several of us climbed up on stools and peaked over the cubbyhole shelf out the window as paramedics and then black and white cars, possibly from the county, arrived one-by-one. Paramedics were quickly pulled away from the lifeless bodies by the people from the black and white cars. The officials went back to their cars and waited until a van arrived. Out of that van came four or five investigators who looked like space beings to the few preschool children sneaking a peak through the windows.

They had protective suits on and breathing masks, apparently knowing very well what kind of danger might await them if they approached the tire and the bodies of our friends and playmates. The bodies were loaded into the van and the "spacemen" used tongs to pick the remaining pieces off the tire and put them into closed glass jars which they repeatedly would stare at as they hauled everything away.

Mrs. Junney tried to arrange activities and a snack as we waited for the authorities to declare it safe to go outside. Then our parents would be allowed to pick us up and take us to homes we now longed for as we feared that also we might fall prey to the things that killed Jazon, April and Choi. My father Gareth Groff arrived that afternoon and Mrs. Junney told him everything while weeping. He remembered the story I had told him only one week earlier – the story that he just couldn't believe.

     ⊱ ⊰ ⊱

To this day nobody knows what these organisms were or what they are properly called. They are not in any scientific books nor have any cryptozoology writers published the information they may be in possession of. The preschool was closed for more than two weeks as county and government officers examined the area and tried to determine if it was safe to have children there. But 12th Street Preschool was not the only location in Harper where pieces had been seen and done damage.

We attended Jazon's funeral and were supposed to attend April's too. But the family was in very poor mental condition and decided to have a closed, private gathering. Choi's parents talked extensively to my parents since I had been present and seen the things that attacked and killed their only son. Choi's father wanted every detail and, as my father put it, was ready to embark on a lifelong quest to find the answers to why and how this could have occurred.

It was Choi's father who informed all of the other parents some months later when city and county government began to stop drilling and cap all of the oil wells in the western district of Harper. He had received information from a friend who was a detective with the Harper Police Department. The official theory of where the organisms called pieces had originated was moving in a subterranean direction. Perhaps someone had been reading historical documents or the ridiculed geological notes of Dr. Avery Gohrn who was long since dead.

The pieces disappeared as quickly as they had arrived. The scars that ruined my childhood and that of many of my preschool mates and the lives of their parents have never gone away. I don't think I ever saw Mrs. Junney smile after that day and Mrs. Morel seemed to lose interest in the preschool eventually moving far away – as far away from Harper as she could.

The *LA Interloper* – a newspaper that claims to cover our county, but whose Los Angelino journalists hate to even set foot in it – turned the epidemic of pieces that was unlike anything any of us had seen into a possible freak swarm of "Africanized bees from Mexico" which had "killed three children, one adult and probably more than fifty dogs and cats" – all in Harper. My father cursed as he read the freak bee attack story. Most of us didn't care anymore. The damage was already done.

6

ENEMY IN THE PARK
1978

Tivoli Days was a veritable obsession for me and many other kids in Harper. But for some reason most of the kids in my sixth grade class at Christ Almighty Elementary didn't give a damn about it. My best friend, Rick Neigh who had lived on Oaf Street near Aunt Jessica had died about a year earlier and – partly as a result of that event – I had been held back one year. I had also become less social and only recently started to hang around with three boys who were two years younger than me. They didn't even attend Christ Almighty; they were public school kids – the type of kids my mother compulsively warned me about.

But they were fun to be with. And they were now the only friends I had in the world. I wasn't about to become a snob.

May had arrived and soon Tivoli Days and the carnival with all of its rides and attractions would too. Rick Kallander was quickly becoming my new best friend. He was actually from the older east district of Harper which is filled with charming California bungalows from the 1930's. He was slightly chubby and had a black crew cut which looked as if he dyed his hair. And that is precisely what he was always teased about at Opal Public School on Crocker Street.

They called him "Slick Rick". He constantly bit his nails and would literally torture his mother to death about clothes which she had already washed, but which he suspected she hadn't. I would always try to change the subject when their bickering started to heat up. Ruthie, Rick's mother, was an overenergetic, fiery foul-mouth who not only looked the part of the stereotypical 1970's nurse; but was one. "Look me in the eye, you snot-nosed brat!" she would often scream with a Brooklyn accent from the doorway to Rick's room when they had a fight.

August Ambrose was more forlorn – a disposition I could very much appreciate as of late. He was extremely thin, almost frail, with dark circles around his eyes and an eagle-like nose. His dishwater blonde hair was shaggy. So we often called him "Shaggy". Augie was constantly writing poems about death. Nobody wanted to hear them, but I tolerated several readings a week. Maybe that's what he most liked about me.

Shaggy would often visit Mrs. Hanson and beg her to tell

him some of Harper's horrible stories. There were plenty to tell.

So with Shaggy we had a veritable Edgar Allen Poe and a backup copy of Mrs. Hanson at our service if needed. And, indeed, this summer that information would prove invaluable.

Paul Chandler was the son of a Harper policeman and acted like one himself. His eyes were so far-set we used to call him the "Cicada". If he screwed up or said something we didn't think was very funny, we would all make a buzzing sound to tease him. To be honest, the brown-haired, thick-lipped kid wasn't that bright. And he was way too domineering. But I'm not going to knock the dead. He was a good kid and he was our friend.

"Cat-eyes" was my nickname. I have grey, droopy, hooded eyes and jet black hair. In fact, I look nothing like my parents, in my opinion. But that's beside the point. Slick, Shaggy and Cicada always teased me and said that my eye-color and shape gave the impression that I also had vertical pupils like a cat. Thus, the nickname.

In early May 1978 our gang – Slick, Shaggy, Cicada and Cat-eyes – was intact and ready to take on the world.

If I had known Harper better, given my previous life experiences, I would have understood that it was not to last — that at the very least Harper would give our gang one hell of a beating and a bloody nose before the summer was out.

৶ ৶ ৶

"Dad?" Paul Chandler cried from his room when he heard that his father had come from the shower.

"What is it now?!" has father yelled back with irritation in his voice while tightening the white bath towel around his waist and walking toward the master bedroom. "Well?" he continued. He was now standing in the doorway of his son's bedroom.

"Is it true that a monster sabotaged the rides at the Tivoli Days carnival last year and the year before?" Paul asked while sitting on the edge of his bed with a scrapbook of newspapers clippings — some of them apparently about the incidents in question. His father now looked even more irritated as he perceived that Paul may have overheard him talking about the case with Paul's mother.

"I don't think it's anything you need to worry about," Paul's father finally replied after a short pause. "It was a very bad person," he continued emphasizing the last word.

"Well then, if it was a person why were people who saw it saying it was the wolfman thing?" Paul argued while giving his father a look which clearly stated that he didn't believe the explanation.

"What wolfman thing?!" Paul's father shouted with exasperation. "Who have you..." his father started off before barging forth and ripping the scrapbook out of his son's hands. "I see!" he exclaimed with a triumphant tone. "Well this explains it!" Paul's father began looking through the scrapbook and then examined the insides of the covers. He closed the scrapbook with a small bang and put it under his arm.

"Dad!" Paul protested and stood up from the bed. "That's Shaggy's scrapbook, I have to give it back tomorrow!" he continued now trying to wrest the edge of the book from his father's armpit.

Paul's father only tightened his grip and backed away. "No problem, son!" he yelled as he turned around. "I'll give it back to Shaggy personally. In fact, maybe I'll pay Mrs. Hanson a visit and leave it there for Shaggy to pick up!"

Paul began to panic and had a lump in his throat for betraying Shaggy, who had reluctantly allowed him to borrow the scrapbook over the weekend. And now Mrs. Hanson who confided in Shaggy was also in for some ridicule from Paul's father. He felt ashamed.

Both Shaggy and Slick were so angry with Cicada on Monday that they didn't speak to him for half of the day. Cicada stood all by himself at recess and sulked while staring through the links of the school's chain-link fence. When I showed up in the afternoon to walk with them to the dime store, they all met up with me by the curb on Crocker Street.

"Hey, Cat-eyes!" they called to me as I approached.

"Guess who's a traitor?" asked Slick.

"I'm not a traitor!!" screamed Cicada, almost in tears.

"Yes you fucking are!!" Shaggy yelled and then gave Cicada a hard shove almost knocking him the ground. He caught his balance just in time not to stumble over the steep curb.

"Why the hell are you all acting screwy?" I asked as I stood between the two warring sides.

"Because they are screwy!!" Cicada retorted bitterly.

"Because this asshole begged to borrow my newspaper clippings album so he could give to his cop father and then pick on old Mrs. Hanson and try to shut her up!!" Shaggy screamed at the top of his lungs so that his words echoed against the school building and other houses.

I turned my head nearly ninety degrees each time trying to listen to both Cicada in back of me and Shaggy in front of me. Cicada started to cry and then confessed "I didn't think my father was so lame that he would take it away!" Cicada was now sobbing outright. The others began to reconsider judging from the expressions on their faces.

"Yeah, well tell Mrs. Hanson that!" Slick finally yelled, indicating that they may have partially forgiven Cicada for the mistake as far as they were concerned, but they were still deeply worried about what Cicada's father might say to Mrs. Hanson. We decided to walk to Mrs. Hanson's cleaning shop instead of the dime store.

"I'll do the talking," Cicada started to boss in his usual manner as things appeared to be returning to normal with the others.

"You've done enough!" retorted Shaggy. "I'll talk to her and tell her how stupid you are!"

"Mellow out, everyone!" I finally yelled exhausted as we hurriedly walked down Crocker and crossed the wide and ever-busy Mercy Shot Boulevard via 13th Street. "I'll try to explain to her what happened and see if she has the album yet," I quipped. We then walked silently toward our destination.

We all began to sweat as we rushed down 13th Street past strip malls, palm trees and used car lots on one of the warmest days of the year to date. The reflection of the sun from the dusty asphalt and concrete was now blindingly bright and made very evident that it was again the season for sun glasses. I donned mine which I had in my shirt pocket and continued our journey.

When we all barged in to Mrs. Hanson's and the welcome bells stopped tinkling, we noticed her red faux bob just above some of the hanging rows of cloths. She was neatly folding towels and sheets. Mrs. Hanson didn't say a word. She must have known that we were there and why. She just shook her head and continued folding laundry.

"Mrs. Hanson…" I said without knowing how to continue. I finally came up with something. "Mrs. Hanson, have you spoken to Mr. … I mean, Detective Chandler today?"

Mrs. Hanson turned around somewhat begrudgingly, looked at us for a few seconds, and then apparently her anger melted. "Kids, I've been speaking to Detective Chandler for more than thirteen years," she finally answered, pronouncing the word "detective" with a slight measure of disdain. She collected the folded towels and sheets, put them into piles and placed them neatly on a rack near the door.

Then she sighed. "He took your album home to your mother, Augie," she told Shaggy. Apparently she had suspected that might alarm him, but now he looked relieved. His mother wasn't nearly as smallminded as Cicada's father.

"Mrs. Hanson, I'm so sorry!" Shaggy said almost in tears and then ran past hanging coats and ironing boards and hugged her. She put her arms around him.

Cicada immediately chimed in. "I'm really sorry too! I should have never let my dad see it!" He then ran to Mrs. Hanson and Shaggy and she opened her right arm to make room for two very sorry boys to hug her.

Now I was beginning to wonder what this entire episode was about. I hadn't had time to even think about it while I was trying to contain the fighting and find a solution. I asked Mrs. Hanson what exactly the problem was.

"Paul's dad worked on the case last year and the year before that, the case of those murders at the Tivoli Days carnival," she commenced.

"I thought it was an accident or that somebody from the people who run the rides got arrested and everything was ok now" I interrupted.

"No..." Mrs. Hanson paused and began to look worried. "I really shouldn't be talking to you kids about this anyway," she said and bit her bottom lip as if warning herself and not us. She was quiet for at least a minute. The silence became unbearable for us.

"Please, Mrs. Hanson!" Shaggy begged, knowing that neither Cicada's nor Slick's parents would ever let them in on what many around town were aware of.

"What's the wolfman thing?" Cicada questioned Mrs. Hanson, recalling the notes and pictures Shaggy had in his album.

"Then you know," Mrs. Hanson said looking right at Cicada. She now looked as though she was ready to give in and talk. Pulling a chair out, she placed it behind the little wooden desk where she would write receipts, slips and count money. Mrs. Hanson then sat down. And we all stood looking at her.

Before she began to speak, she took out a tube of bright red lipstick, quickly redid her lips and then straightened out her simple floral dress. "Harper, children, is not like other cities," she began. She then continued as we stood there in silence listening to her.

"Some people, like the geologist that warned the government about this entire area, believe that there is a world of living things deep beneath our feet that we don't even know about. And since Harper, Daughn,

Huntingdon and Newland Beach sit atop a deep, deep crack or fault in the earth's crust, which extends almost to the surface, they say that these things can sometimes get to the surface and do very bad things to the people that live here," Mrs. Hanson narrated. But then she paused as she saw that Cicada and Slick were starting to look more scared than curious.

"Is that what the pieces were that killed my friends in preschool?" I immediately questioned her after finding a possible answer to why that horrible day happened.

"Yes, Gordie!" she replied almost enthusiastically as though she were a teacher and I had solved a math problem she had given me. "And that's probably what caused your neighbors'... I mean your grandparents' neighbors' house to fall into the ground" she continued, almost appearing to regret mentioning the Tamms' demise to me.

"But does the wolfman thing live underground somewhere?" Shaggy asked.

"That's just one idea, kids," she continued "Nobody really can say. But a policeman who retired told me that there is a theory out there that something about the Translucy..." she stopped and muttered various variations of the name trying to find the right one.

"Translucene!" she finally shouted in victory as she had remembered the correct name of the fault. "The Translucene Fault," she now continued "may somehow cause doors to open between our world and another world, just now and then. And that's when bad things happen in Harper," she concluded.

We each took a candy from Mrs. Hanson's large candy jar and left without saying much of anything to each other. Slick, Shaggy and Cicada went east on 13th Street and I continued west to Federal Prison Avenue and to my parent's house on 14th Street and Liberia Avenue. My mother was in the living room when I came, looking at old pictures. Curiously, they were pictures of Priit and Esther Tamm.

∞ ∞ ∞

"That goddam geologist was crazy as a loon and everybody in the goddamn state knew it!" Grandpa Ahnus screamed at the top of his lungs when Grandma told him what I had confided in her about the Translucene Fault. "The newspaper article said he was schizophrenic and probably drank bootleg, goddammit!"

"Shush! Please, Charles!" Virginia Ahnus begged her husband trying to settle him down as I lay under the covers across from them in the side bedroom shivering with fear that night. They were having one of their infamous, but not uncommon middle-of-the-night brawls as they lay in the master bedroom awake at 2 a.m.

I was staying the night with my grandparents while my mother and father were visiting a filmmaker friend of my father in Mexico. This was the 14th of May and I still had a school day ahead of me. I could just imagine how tired I was going to feel in the morning.

"There are occultists all over this city who have been having secret meetings and conjuring up all kinds of evil crap since the 1950's. That's a hell of a lot more believable than UFO's and monsters from underground!" my grandfather continued his outbreak. "There are faults all over the goddam state and you don't hear of houses falling into them, do you?!" he then yelled.

I didn't know what to believe. It seemed as though everyone had their own theory of why the things that happened in Harper had occurred. Everyone was obviously just guessing. The fighting died down until I fell asleep around 3 a.m.

The following morning the principle announced over the intercom the news that our school would no longer be called "Christ Almighty Elementary"; but instead would now bear the name "Buttercup School". This would take effect from the following schoolyear. My mother later revealed to me what she had heard at the Parent and Teachers Meeting earlier that week.

Since language was changing during the 1970's, the name of our school was beginning to draw jokes and prank calls from people who would taunt the office personnel when they answered the phone, "Christ Almighty". The caller would sometimes answer back "You can say that again!" and then hang up. Other times the prank caller would pretend to rebuke the personnel saying, "I call a Christian elementary school and the first thing I hear is use of the Lord's name in vain! Shame on you!"

The second reason for the name change was that the school was now adding the 7th and 8th grades. We would no longer just be an elementary school. That in turn implied that I had to keep going to the school for two more years. My plans for transferring to Opel School were now dashed.

A couple of days later I walked straight from school to the east side to Slick's house, I could hardly contain my rage during our special meeting as I told Slick, Cicada and Shaggy the bad news. "I don't want to go to Mrs. Butterworth's!" I yelled, making fun of the school's future name as we tried to figure out how I might get out of the new predicament.

"You should just stick it out and stop complaining," said Cicada in his normal bossy police tone. He was certainly going to follow in his father's footsteps with that personality. "You've just gotta hope they don't open up a senior high school before you graduate," he then said in a snide tone and snickered.

"So, it's rice-a-roni with broccoli and summer squash with brown sugar and butter, kids," a voice said from the doorway to Slick's room where we all sat. Slick's mother stood there with laundry in her arms with her usual short bobbed hairstyle and brown hair. She was also wearing the predictable white knit nurse's sweater which seemed to be her signature style – both at home and at work.

"I thought we were gonna have barbeque!" Slick yelled back. I knew what was coming and instinctively began to move my hands toward my ears.

"Listen, you ungrateful weisenheimer," the Brooklyn-accented torrent of expletives shot forth in our direction. "I've worked a ten-hour shift, am doing your goddam laundry for the umpteenth time now and feeding you and your wack friends! Your father can't light the damn grill all the way from New Jersey, so shut your face and gimme that t-shirt!" Mrs. Kallander finished her diatribe.

"Alright, already!" Slick shouted back begrudgingly and then threw the t-shirt from the bed in her general direction. Mrs. Kallander silently picked the t-shirt up off the floor and trudged toward the bathroom in her flip-flops.

Eventually we ate. By then we had hatched a plan for me to get expelled.

      ~6~ ~e~ ~9~

May 21st 1978 is the first day it made itself known to us – beginning with Cicada and Shaggy. They were the first to see it. If I recall correctly, they first saw something – a short person, maybe a midget – running around between the rides which were being assembled in Tivoli Park that day. It was playing a sort of peek-a-boo game with them, they thought. Then they heard it speak for the first time. It could speak to either or both of them. It could show them things, make them do things that they didn't want to do – very bad things. It had even told them things about my family that I didn't know and that I didn't want to believe.

When it finally slowly revealed itself to them, it knew everything about them and it knew what it could threaten them with if they told anyone. Cicada and Shaggy pissed on themselves as they saw the wolfman thing for the first time. How merciful their fate would have been had this incarnation of pure evil merely been a monster or perhaps a mentally warped carnival worker suffering from a disorder like hypertrichosis. But it was so much more than a monster, being extremely intelligent, amoral and able to drive anyone it wished completely and irreparably insane.

This was supposed to be my first day of playing hooky from the school I hated. We were supposed to sit in Tivoli Park all day long and watch the carnival workers assemble the rides for the Tivoli Days carnival which would start the next day. This was something I had always wanted to do.

110

When Cicada and Shaggy came to get me, they were changed. They weren't children anymore. They had lost all of their illusions and all of their innocence. I recognized the look in their eyes, because I had undergone this process in preschool and again the previous year when I saw things that simply should not be. They stood side-by-side staring at me without expression. I didn't know them anymore.

"We've got a meeting to attend," Cicada bossed, speaking in a very cynical tone like that of an adult. I just stared back at them, unsure what to say. "We've got a meeting with the wolfman, and he doesn't like to wait!" Shaggy yelled in a commanding tone. The song "Lido Shuffle" was blaring from the speakers where the carnival workers were going about their routine.

"We're staying here. I'm not going to any meeting," I said firmly.

"You can swallow your human pride or you can enjoy a rubber lampshade moment just like the last friend who died in front of your eyes," an almost effeminate and creepy voice said. This voice was not coming from Cicada or Shaggy. Yet, they appeared to have heard exactly what I had heard, and I had heard it in my head. I felt my bladder releasing as I realized by instinct exactly what kind of adversary was calling the shots now and how far that enemy could and would go.

"Don't fuck with him, Cat," Cicada warned me direly and then made a cutthroat gesture.

I walked with them toward the collection of trailers, trucks and half-assembled carnival rides and we sat down on the benches in the covered enclosure where the hamburgers were always served and people would sit and eat during the carnival. No one else was there. Suddenly I heard rustling from behind a eucalyptus tree near the end of the enclave. For a couple of seconds, I saw the face.

It wasn't a child, a youngster or a midget. It was a small stalky man with blond hair all over. The hair was shorter and sparser on the face. But the face was indeed covered from forehead to neck with short blonde fur. If you looked at the face and tried to imagine what it might look like without the fur, you immediately understood that this was not a human being. It was humanoid, but not completely human.

"Get a good enough look?" I heard it ask in my mind just as I was pondering what it was. "The wolfman thing, of course!" it answered in my head before I could even begin to ask the question "What are you?".

"Porky's in a bad mood today and someone is going to have to pay" we all heard it say in our heads. I knew, because I saw Cicada lip the words and Shaggy suddenly look very scared. Cicada was either losing or had lost his mind.

"What do you want from us?!" I screamed at the eucalyptus tree which was now void of any sign of the wolfman thing. There was only silence.

"You'll see!" we finally heard in our heads. I could then see something childishly running across the park and hiding behind trees, occasionally poking its hairy face and yellowish bug eyes into view. Cicada was in some kind of trance whispering to himself. Shaggy and I knew we needed to get ahold of his parents, even if it meant that we were now in deep trouble.

"Let's go to the old bookstore and use Mrs. Kariis' telephone!" I said to Shaggy. "We need to get help!"

We tried to pull Cicada along with us, but he was completely oblivious to everything now. So we had him sit back down on one of the benches in the enclosure. At Mrs. Kariis' bookstore we panicked and told the incredulous 59-year-old, who looked at us over her glasses, what had happened.

"Settle down and I will call Mr. Chandler at the police department" she finally proposed. Mrs. Kariis didn't believe a word of anything we had said, except that Cicada was having some kind of psychological episode. That's what she told Detective Chandler as they spoke for nearly twenty minutes. Cicada's father arrived within ten minutes after the call finished. Then my mother and Shaggy's father arrived – both utterly infuriated.

"Kuidas sa mulle midagi sellist julged tehda?!" (How dare you do this to me!) my mother started off in Estonian, taking me by the arm out the bookstore door and to the car.

"Koolist popitegemine on kuritegelik!" (Playing hooky is criminal!) Mrs. Kariis hollered in Estonian, looking firmly and pointing at me.

My mother now remembered that Mrs. Kariis was also of Estonian heritage and just about fainted with added embarrassment as she jerked me, opened the car door and pushed me in. Shaggy disappeared into his father's Roadrunner, and his father burnt rubber down Mercy Shot Boulevard. As my mother and I drove slowly past Tivoli Park we could just see paramedics and Cicada's father standing around where he had been sitting when we left him. That was the last I ever saw of him.

On May 21st 1978, the first day of the Tivoli Days carnival I was grounded and forbidden to attend the carnival. Maybe that saved my life. The phone rang in the afternoon and my mother began to cry after she had hung up. My father came back early from a meeting with a client and sat silently on the couch. I was afraid to ask either of them anything since they were so mad at me. But they eventually decided to talk to me.

"Paul Chandler and his family are dead," my mother said while looking down with wet eyes. I didn't say a word. I couldn't even think of a word to say.

114

"How…" I started after a minute or two.

"How did he…?" I tried to continue while tears were welling up.

"No," my mother said quietly and shook her head. She wasn't going to tell me how.

Paul Chandler, an eleven-year-old, had stolen one of his father's powerful guns which was stored in a safe protected by a combination which only his father presumably knew and had then shot his mother and his father. He had subsequently left the house and entered an off-limits transformer station on Crocker Street where he climbed up onto the structure and was electrocuted.

On the 22nd of May 1978, the second day of the Tivoli Days carnival two people were thrown from the cart inside of the "Ghost Train" ride after being dowsed with water. They fell onto the electrified tracks which power the carts and were in flames by the time carnival workers managed to cut off the current. People stuck inside the ride didn't dare get out of their stalled carts as blue sparks shot about and the stench of ozone and burning flesh and smoke filled the air.

Amid all the ruckus and screaming they saw a figure standing inside, occasionally illuminated by the blue fire and sparks. It was a short, stalky creature with short hair all over. And it was smiling at all of them fiendishly.

Rescue workers recovered what appeared to have been a boy with black hair and a woman, about forty, with brown hair who was wearing a white knit sweater with a nurse's pin from a nursing school in New York City. The bodies and rest of the clothes were badly burned, and dental records were being sought. The police department and government investigators were baffled as there should have been an automatic power cutoff and an electrical surge up to 60 000 volts should not have been possible. This was the second year in a row that such a mass murder had happened on this ride, and the killer had still not been caught.

Shaggy moved with his parents that same year to another state. Our gang — Slick, Shaggy, Cicada and Cat-eyes — was no more. Harper and its monsters had once again defeated any hopes for a normal life.

7

INCIDENT AT ROD'S BIG BURGER
1979

Harper still lives in the 1950's. Everything about the city reveals this fact. Maybe it is because people in Harper are sleepwalking through life, not interested in renewal or changes. Many residents still cling to their memories of a time when there was hope and security, when family and neighbors were part of their lives. They try to live within these memories, attempting to re-live an era when reality was simple, safe and monsters didn't seem to exist.

From the straight and boring streets lined with utility poles, palm trees, carob trees, Norfolk Island pines and eucalyptus trees you can see strip malls, drive-in restaurants, gas stations and two-story apartment buildings. For as far as the eye can see, there is asphalt, concrete and buildings with plain white façades only occasionally adorned with an exposed stone veneer – all below a veritable spider's web of crisscrossing utility lines. A random mini-lawn, some trees and flower beds in front of public buildings and houses in mid-century style break the monotony of this little section of a southern California mega-oasis trying to deny that it is part and parcel of a dry and barren desert. Flower beds in town are typically graced with the seemingly obligatory presence of agave, wild rye, ice plant and paradise plants – homely but hardy vegetation growing above a stingy layer of reddish terracotta chips.

The Googie architecture of Harper's diners, cinemas, bowling halls, gas stations and grocery stores speaks of a time when the city seemed to have the world on a platter and a promising future. But then a once ultramodern style unceremoniously ripened into a tacky and outdated eyesore. The cityscape that my family, friends and I grew up with ultimately became a mere curiosity for outsiders and something most Harperites don't even think about.

There would be a small uprising of sorts against this stagnation in the early 1980's as some homeowners spent money to make believe that their houses were not single-family clones built in the 1950's. These few dissidents – most of them originally from elsewhere – added wooden façades, fireplaces and second stories. In town, some businesses and public buildings would eventually be outfitted with phony Spanish façades and terracotta tile roofs.

This was little more than a half-baked attempt to hide the local secret – the backward-looking reverie of the collective fugue state most Harperites knew and needed but which outsiders simply wouldn't understand or be impressed by. True Harperites continued – untouched by the limited architectonic insurrection – to live in the Harper we had always known.

Even as late as 1979 Rod's Big Burger remained true to its 1950's style – the exposed stone veneer, the typical mid-century flower bed, the slanting Googie shape of the diner itself. For my entire life and probably most of my parents' Rod's had had the same look – both inside and outside. And ever since they had met in the 1950's, the Ahnus, Groff and Tamm families would converge on Rod's diner where we would all assemble for lively dinner discussions in Estonian mixed with English. Nearly all important occasions were commemorated at Rod's Big Burger with steak dinners, hot fudge cake and lots of scalding hot coffee. I miss those days.

The dinners and occasions at Rod's ceased when the Tamm's disappeared into that hole in 1972. The Tamm's house was partially rebuilt, but still vacant – a standing monument to the painful void in our lives and in our community. From the time I began swimming lessons at the public pool near Tivoli Park, Rod's became the go-to source for hamburgers to gorge on after practice. My grandparents would drive me there. And we would sit in the car outside Rod's in front of the long row of brown-tinted diner windows just behind the flowerbeds while we enjoyed hamburgers, french-fries and cherry colas. Even this had become a tradition. And even this tradition ended in a nightmare.

The 2nd of July, 1979 began as a very normal day. On that particular day I didn't have swimming practice, but we had decided to drive across town to Rod's Big Burger and eat after running some errands with my grandparents. When we all climbed into the "Brown Clown" – as my sister Marina had dubbed my grandfather's old four-door Dodge sedan – it was a cool and sunny morning. The grass was still covered with dew which reflected the lime-colored morning sunlight.

Grandpa Ahnus began his usual ritual by stepping three times on the gas pedal before he turned the key in the ignition. Black exhaust shot from the tailpipe as he revved the engine and we backed out of the garage. The automatic, remote-controlled garage door closed as we backed onto Ballistic Avenue and turned on 14th street and again on Federal Prison Avenue. This was the standard protocol that I had witnessed hundreds if not thousands of times.

As the familiar journey continued and we drove down 13th Street past Helmet Center toward Mercy Shot Boulevard and the eastern district of Harper, I thought about the Tamm's who were no longer. When we passed Tivoli Park an inevitable moment arrived as it did every time we passed Tivoli Park – I thought about Cicada, Slick and Shaggy. My grandmother had told me, each time I cried and remembered the events of 1978, that regardless of what had taken my friends away from me, it could never take their meaning and memory away. So I always remembered them and paid my respects mentally when we drove by this sinister historical landmark.

As we drove down Crocker Street toward Laguna Center the reflection of sunlight from the dusty concrete and asphalt was almost blinding. Both my grandmother and I put on our sunglasses. The chimes of the Madonna Church on East 12th street could be heard, meaning that it was noon. Traffic was now lively. And older men with thinning slicked-back hair and short-sleeved dress shirts were making their rounds – some to cash social security checks, others to walk up to the windows of parked cars and ask other retirees like my grandfather if they could spare a dime.

The Brown Clown and its passengers came to a halt under the skimpy branches of a carob tree in front of the various shops at Laguna Center. We had parked in front of the dime store where Cicada, Slick, Shaggy and I had spent many memorable moments playing with toys and reading comic books in the aisles. Mr. Crockle, the owner, never minded. We usually bought something at least once a week. It was one of those good memories that was still vivid for me. I smiled.

When Grandpa Ahnus jumped back into the car after visiting the post office and bank we were off to Rod's Big Burger and to the luscious burgers I never grew tired of. We parked near the entrance and my grandfather confirmed that we wanted the usual food and drinks. There were cars, but no people in the parking lot. No one was entering the diner and no one was leaving. This was unusual for Rod's. Because of the cars, we knew they couldn't be closed. But things were eerily quiet.

Without any further reflection Grandpa Ahnus left, shut the car door and disappeared into the entrance. We waited the usual ten minutes. And then it all started.

My grandmother was tracing the rims of her sunglasses and tapping the lenses, slightly bored, when the sound of muffled screaming began to resound from inside Rod's Big Burger. It was as if every single customer had started screaming at the top of their lungs in terror. Then came the sound of breaking glasses and plates followed by more screaming. My heart began to pound. Something was not right.

"What is going on in there?" my grandmother asked as we both strained to see through the brown-tinted windows of the diner from the car. Apparently no one was sitting in the booths near the windows. We had hardly come to this realization when the door to the diner entrance flew open so violently that it crashed against the stopper. We could hear the bang from inside the car.

It was Grandpa Ahnus. He was rushing away from the entrance and toward the car past the newspaper dispensers faster than I had ever seen him move. The fear in his eyes as he grabbed the door and violently pulled it open was enough to put both my grandmother and I into panic mode. He had never had this look in his eyes.

"It's coming out!!" he screamed like a child with night terrors as he tried to start the car as fast as he could.

"Charles, what's coming out? What are you talking about?" my grandmother asked with fear and confusion in her voice.

"What's going on in there?" I then asked, when he kept trying to start the car and didn't answer my grandmother.

"Just shut up goddam it – both of you!!" he screamed in total panic as the motor finally started and exhaust blocked the view in back of us.

The car motor had barely started when the door to the entrance flew open again – this time, so violently that the glass in the door shattered. I couldn't believe my eyes when I saw what was running from the entrance toward the car. My grandmother and I instinctively pushed the pegs down to lock our doors as fast as we could. Then we checked to see whether I had locked the door furthest from me in the back.

We didn't have time for anything else. I got a very good look at what was pursuing Grandpa Ahnus and now us when it hopped onto the hood of the car and began trying to break the windshield. It first began to examine my grandmother after managing to start a series of cracks in the glass. Then it quickly looked at me.

The black, leather-like skin was shiny and reflected the sun as the thing crawled up over the top of the car. The pounding sound moved over and then behind us as the horrendous eyes and head reappeared upside down in the rear window. Now it was trying to break the rear window and get to me in the back seat. I hopped onto the floor in front of the rear seat and huddled in terror as far away as possible from the yellowish eyes which resembled those of a ring-necked duck. The rear window cracked and Grandpa pushed the gas to the floor and the Brown Clown instantly into forward drive.

We had been backing away from the diner like a bat out of hell as the thing tried to break both the front and rear windows of the car. Now the change of direction threw the trim and aggressive humanoid monster off the car and to the asphalt in the parking lot. It got right up unscathed and hopped back onto the rear of the car. I could see that a single blow was all that was needed to completely shatter the cracked rear window. After that there would be nothing between me and the implausible fiend that had appeared out of nowhere. Grandpa threw the Brown Clown into reverse again, trying to repeat his previous success.

124

This time it didn't work.

The creature shattered the rear window. And the pieces of glass flew at me and my grandparents like snow blowing horizontally in a snowstorm. Apparently, the creature needed to make some sort of perverse victory cry before it ripped me and my grandparents to shreds. It let out a bloodcurdling and bizarre sound not unlike that of a wild donkey as I climbed over the front seat and squished myself between my grandparents who were already unlocking their doors. They clearly anticipated the need to quickly escape the car once the creature climbed into it.

For the first time, I could see people running from the main entrance to Rod's. As we waited for the creature to climb through the hole where the rear window had been, we could see a man in a blue shirt and jeans running toward the car. He was holding a revolver and had it pointed toward the creature. Grandpa Ahnus looked back to see if the creature was in the car yet. But it had now caught sight of the man with the gun and backed out, hopping to the asphalt from the rear hood of the car.

The Brown Clown wasn't running anymore. Either it had stalled or Grandpa Ahnus had shut it down. We sat still on the glass-covered seat as the creature — which had a bizarre protrusion like the heel of a high-heel shoe on the front of its head — readied itself to attack the would-be hero.

The man in the blue shirt fired a warning shot in the air which meant absolutely nothing to the leathery miscreant. It charged right toward him.

Another shot ripped through the air and echoed between the one and three-story buildings near Rod's Big Burger. This shot had been point blank and thrust the creature backward. Then it continued forward toward the shooter unharmed. Two more shots echoed as my grandparents and I – together with the few hostages still standing outside of Rod's – looked on in disbelief. This was clearly not a man in a suit.

The creature jumped the man who had tried to save our lives so that both fell to the pavement. Despite its exotic nature, which the terrified onlookers could only fearfully speculate about, it knew very well how to break a human neck. It did so quickly and efficiently. The man who had tried to save our lives lay on the asphalt with his head facing forward – from his back. Hope was now lost and help was obviously not on its way.

A creature unlike the horrors that even I had seen during my life had appeared out of nowhere, taken restaurant guests and personnel hostage and murdered people. It was immune to bullets from a powerful revolver. More than thirty people had seen the monster with their own eyes. Grandpa Ahnus was shaking, silent and as white as a sheet.

Out of nowhere came another phenomenon without motive or explanation. An ultra-low but very loud sound – a drone as though someone had started to draw a bow against a mile-long acoustic base string – resonated for about a minute. The eerie sound was so powerful and low that people could feel it in their bodies and windows rattled.

When the sound stopped, the creature was completely gone, nowhere to be found. The sky which had been blue was now suddenly white, perhaps covered by high clouds. The town was bathed in an eerie greyish hue as though everything were part of a 1950's black and white movie.

Perhaps effected by the events and the sound, my grandparents and I were weak in our legs and arms and shivering. We had to wait a few minutes before standing up. As we slowly and carefully left the car and looked around us at the carnage, we noticed that former hostages and witnesses were suffering from the same effect – many of them sitting down on the ledges of the flowerbed or supporting themselves against the newspaper dispensers in front of the entrance. What had happened here? we asked ourselves. The sound of sirens – lots of them – grew until police, paramedics and black cars with white license plates finally arrived.

❦   ❧   ❧

Both of my grandparents required a hospital stay of three days for observation after the incident. Despite being weak and having an irregular heartbeat, my grandfather tried to answer questions from police and government officials who were dodgy about their credentials. The police told Grandpa Ahnus that they would appreciate it if he cooperated with the other officials. Then it was my turn to answer their questions. People in Harper were starting to call my grandfather a hero for having dared to leave the restaurant and for distracting the perpetrator so that others could escape from the diner.

My grandfather would then get angry and tell them about the man in the blue shirt who had tried to save our lives and kill the creature. Grandpa Ahnus reminded them that the unnamed man had given his life for others. Still, they continued to propagate the version where Grandpa had saved everyone's lives.

The first thing my grandfather had done when the incident was over was to vomit for more than thirty minutes. Then he was taken to Newland Beach Memorial Hospital for observation. No person or organization ever claimed responsibility for the murders and the officials that interviewed everyone who had been present never got back to anyone with an update on the progress of their investigation. They had promised to do so.

Something from somewhere with black, shiny skin like a leather jacket and yellow eyes like a ring-necked duck had appeared at Rod's Big Burger and taken personnel and guests hostage. The head cook Frank Tadia had gone for his gun and was going to shoot it. That was a bad move on Tadia's part as the creature grabbed him, dragged him back into the kitchen and fried his face on the kitchen grill. My grandfather had seen this through the kitchen service window behind the cash register. And he, like many others, had heard the horrible screaming and smelt the results. That was enough to convince everyone to stay put – except for Grandpa.

A barrage of letters from former hostages, their families and others wanting answers arrived at city hall and government agencies various and sundry. No answers were offered and the *LA Interloper* began to speculate that it might have been a terrorism incident linked to the crisis in Iran. Lots of nasty letters to the editor from those who were present followed. Some of them were even published.

Virginia Ahnus developed a debilitating nervous tick after the incident and Charles Ahnus never drove again. My grandparents began, for the first time since the 1950's, to consider moving away from Harper to Laguna Beach. They had seen enough.

8

VICTIMS OF THE RED MASK
1977

Rick Neigh was my best friend, and he lived on Oaf Street just short of the steep hill that descends toward the posh little enclave city of Daughn. We had been friends for many years and had met in third grade at Christ Almighty Elementary school. One day – shortly after school had started and while I was staying the weekend at Aunt Jessica's house – I saw him playing ball with an older kid in the middle of Oaf Street. I realized that he lived in my neighborhood. From then on mutual visits and overnighters were a weekend staple.

When Rick was together with his older friend, Rodney Gillcairn, they regularly teased and taunted me. But when Rodney wasn't around, Rick and I were nearly inseparable. So I always tried to make sure Rodney wasn't with Rick when he came to my house or when I visited his house.   That wasn't always possible. Sometimes Rick hid Rodney at his house when I was supposed to come over and visit. That way they knew I would arrive and they could then gang up on me. This didn't happen very often. But when it did happen, they always had something in store for me – something they knew I wouldn't like at all.

One time they had stumbled upon a nest of spiders in the Gulch – the wild and overgrown little canyon just west of Harper and south of Daughn and which was officially off limits to hikers and visitors. Both of them knew that I was frightened of spiders. So they put a bunch of them in jars, brought them home and let them loose in one of the bedrooms at Rick's house. Then they forced me into that bedroom where between eight and ten spiders the size of golf balls were scurrying around disturbed and disoriented. I left through the bedroom window – which I broke in pure terror – and didn't speak to Rick for three months. But fences were gradually mended as they had been many times before.

Rick and I were polar opposites. Where I was dark-haired and skinny, Rick was light blonde and muscular. My hooded and drooping grey eyes were countered in Rick by a pair of brown, open eyes which looked as though they constantly longed for adventure. Rick always had a crew cut and wore tank tops. I always had the same short-but-clean hairstyle and wore the same Hang-Ten striped shirts.

For Rick, nothing short of the latest designer tennis shoes was worth even considering. For me, clothes and shoes weren't important as long as I had the basics. People and my family were paramount for me. Rick was athletic. I was not.

You may wonder – as many have – why on earth I befriended someone like Rick and stuck with him for years. The logic of a third-grader is a mystery of its own. Indeed, I really can't tell you how I reasoned back then. We were close much of the time. Yet we were rivals part of the time – predictably, when Rodney was around.

Because Rick and Rodney were likely to try to terrorize me with it, I didn't tell either of them when I noticed what was scurrying around between the piles of junk in the side bedroom at my house. Even my slender and alert Siamese cat Lill could sense what was in that room. At first, she was curious about something behind the door to the bedroom – a room which was merely used to store the things that we didn't really want; but which we couldn't bring ourselves to discard. But then Lill stopped clawing at the door and wanting someone to open it. Instead, she would stand outside the side bedroom door with the hair raised up on her back, sometimes hissing at the crack between the door and the floor.

My mother thought it was a mouse. She would open the door sometimes, telling me that the best thing to do was to let the cat do her job and get rid of the pest.

I knew better. And so my mother would open the door and I would close the door. We would then fight about it – sometimes in Estonian, sometimes in English, depending upon whether my father was home. She insisted that I had seen a mouse or a rat running between the boxes of junk and taking cover under an old dresser. I was adamant that I had seen something else scurrying and hiding under that dresser.

Then our mother told Marina about the dispute and Marina – as often was the case – turned it all into a joke. I would wake up some mornings when my sister was visiting us and see Marina in the doorway of the back bedroom, which was my room. She would be standing there wearing a cheap, paper mask depicting a killer clown and making creepy noises.

She thought this paper mask was the one that I had told our mother about – the mask that I had seen scurrying around like some deformed reptile between the boxes of junk in the side bedroom. I was protective of my older sister and let her think that the clown mask was the one I was afraid of. I didn't want her looking for the red mask.

I was into facing my fears long before I ever started seeing my psychiatrist Dr. Woodward as an adult. In fact, one afternoon after school in 1977 I decided to go into that musty side bedroom that reeked of mold and other moisture damage. The sunlight was always very strong through the window of the infamous white junk room – despite the cheap, yellowing roller blinds that apparently solely served to hide the state of affairs in that room from our next door neighbors.

There was no one else home. Even Lill was into the habit of staying outside for as long a she could as if to avoid the house as much as possible. I had decided to get the distasteful chore done while the room was well-lit. So I walked down the dimly-lit hallway of our one-family house – a clone of my grandparent's house next door and up the hill. The door to the side bedroom was always swollen and needed a decent shove to open.

Once that was accomplished, the dank odor and brightness of the room hit me head-on. I knew my task: I was to find and closely examine the red mask I had erroneously perceived to be scurrying around and see for myself that it was just a rubber mask with no life of its own. Then I would be cured of my fear. If there was any danger of injury, then it was most certainly from all of the junk which I might stumble over in this parlor of chaos and disarray.

It wasn't long before I had located the object of my fear. The mask was no longer under the dresser. Had Marina inadvertently plucked it out from the under the dresser when she was looking for the other mask? I wondered. Regardless, it was now laying in one of the very narrow clearings between the stacks of boxes close to the bedroom closet. I approached with caution.

The red mask was absolutely hideous. It was the color of light blood and didn't look like any monster or character I had ever seen on television or in comic books. It consisted of a horrible face and a cap-like extension to hold it onto the wearer so that no cheap rubber band was needed. There was no color variation and everything was made of the same rubbery material. There were only two openings for the very narrow eyes and a small one for the hideous, thick-lipped mouth. I certainly never bought or used a mask like this for Halloween. And Marina would hardly have donned such an abomination for Halloween when she was living at home. Where had it come from? Who had bought it? I wondered in fear and confusion. Was it perhaps something that Rick or Rodney had left at my house long ago when they were visiting? I deliberated.

The mask didn't smell right, either. Instead of the typical sour latex smell that I was used to, it reeked of a combination of leather, latex and musk. And when I moved in closer to examine the material, I was happy that I hadn't decided to touch the mask or put it on. For whatever company had produced this monstrosity must have been unusually obsessed with detail.

On close examination I could see small capillaries running through the material of the mask. While trying to determine the point of such detail in an otherwise plain and unicolor item, I saw movement. The middle of the face sank toward the floor as the narrow holes where the eyes should be opened slightly. Mesmerized with terror and wanting to doubt that I was interpreting the movement correctly, I backed away keeping an eye on the red mask. It was then I caught site of the mouth. The thick lips where rhythmically opening and closing in an increasingly more violent manner.

In less than a second, I had bolted away, out the bedroom doorway and into the dark hall, slamming the door and making sure that it was fully closed. I stood frozen on the other side, grasping the round doorknob and listening to the surreal sounds of squeaking and crackling as the mask scurried around between the boxes – perhaps toward the door. Then the sound of my own pounding heart drowned out every other noise.

When my mother came home from working at the Two Guys department store in Daughn, I told her what had happened. Of course, she didn't believe a word.

"Gordon!" she yelled as she sat on the couch removing her work shoes "I'm tired and I don't have time for your little horror stories!"

"It's not a horror story; it's the truth!" I yelled. "I don't want to sleep here tonight with that thing just in the next room," I told my mother.

"If this doesn't stop soon, Gordon, we are going to have to find a doctor who can deal with you," my mother said looking at me intently, but with a smattering of faux concern.

"So, you think I'm crazy!" I yelled "You all thought I was crazy in preschool with those things. And then three kids died!" I bellowed at my mother, looking at her with disdain.

My mother's look changed to one which expected me to draw my own conclusions from the statement I had just made. "Exactly," she finally pointed out. "That may be what has set you off about the mask in the bedroom," she proposed.

"Whatever!" I barked. "Can I stay with Grandpa and Grandma tonight?" I asked, fearing that the answer would be negative. My fear was confirmed.

All through the night I could hear my parents awake and having their own version of a crisis meeting in the living room. My mother made intermittent calls to Marina and consulted my sister in Estonian. "Mida sa arvad, kallis?" (What do you think, dear?) echoed over and over again down the hallway, as my mother acted like Marina was a psychologist or doctor with a hotline.

My sister had moved out in 1975 and now lived in Daughn with her well-to-do Italian husband Michele.

She was learning her part as a Daughnite very well and currently wanted little to do with our Harper-based family's internal problems. So I doubt my mother received much advice from my snobby sister. Even if she had, it wouldn't have been of much help. My dear mother was blissfully unaware that in less than a week, both she and my father would be the ones in need of psychiatric assistance.

   ⁝ ⁝ ⁝

School was finally out. The smell of honeysuckles filled the air in most of our neighborhood. People were out walking in groups or with baby strollers and dogs on leashes. My plans were made. It was Saturday the 11th of June, 1977. Rick Neigh had promised me that he would come to my house alone and that we would sneak into the Gulch and look for unknown, hidden treasures there. We had the entire summer in front of us, and I was looking forward to long, interesting days with Rick and with my grandparents. I had also started swimming lessons at the public pool near Tivoli Park.

When I caught sight of that fat slob with long, blonde hair and a t-shirt that didn't even cover the gut that was sticking out in front, just above a pair of grey sweatpants,

I knew this was a bad omen. Rodney Gilcairn was cycling slowly beside Rick who was walking toward my house. I seriously considered going back inside and shutting the door. But they had both seen me on the porch in front of the blue and white lathed plaster house. Besides, they would have never let me hear the end of it, probably even broken into my house somehow.

Rodney pushed the stand down on his ten-speed bicycle. He was planning on coming in with Rick. And I knew what that meant.

"Rick and I have plans today," I said with an expression directed toward Rodney that indicated he wasn't welcome.

"Yeah," he answered back with a smirk. "and we have plans for you today, Gordie," he snidely remarked, pushing me to the side as they both went into my living room. My mother and father weren't home yet and weren't expected for another hour. They made their way to the kitchen and took two of my parent's beers out of the refrigerator. After pulling the tabs and drinking straight from the beer cans, they burped and proceeded into the living room where they both plopped themselves down on our couch.

"So, Gordie-boy, what are we going to do today?" Rodney asked, taking another sip of bear and spilling some on the leather couch. Rick was giggling.

My main objective was now to get both of them out of my house. In order to lure them away, I suggested that we go the Gulch. If we got far enough away outside, I could always run back home and lock the door, I strategized.

"Yeah, well we can all go to the Gulch when we've finished our tour of your house, Gordie-boy," Rodney proposed spitefully.

"We're not doing a tour of my house," I replied "My parents don't allow strangers to look around at our stuff," I pleaded with warm cheeks and a growing anger.

"Yeah, but your parents aren't here right now!" Rodney countered and then took a huge gulp of beer before slamming the nearly empty can down on the coffee table and getting up to start the forced tour of my home.

Both of them proceeded down the hallway, despite my protests. The first stop was my parents' bedroom – the master bedroom opposite the side bedroom and which corresponded exactly to the master bedroom of my grandparent's home. When Rodney Gilcairn started fishing my mother's underwear out of the drawers and putting it on his head and laughing, I looked at Rick. Despite my pleading glance, Rick did nothing to stop the desecration of my home. I was hurting deeply as they proceeded to the bedroom across the hall – the side bedroom.

140

Now, for the first time, Rodney was tripped up and confused. He had opened the door to the bright room and seen a landscape of total confusion – cardboard boxes and unopened gift packages from the 1950's arranged like skyscrapers. He turned and looked back at Rick and me, shaking his head.

"Fuck, man!" he exclaimed. "Look at all this junk! When was the last time your mother cleaned – 1904?" he editorialized. Then he went into the room and immediately located something to taunt me with. Disappearing behind one of the cardboard skyscrapers, he quickly reappeared and charged toward the doorway where Rick and I were standing.

"Boo!!!" Rodney screamed wearing the red mask and hoping to scare us. He did. We hopped backward. And then I started to order him to take the mask off immediately for his own safety. Rick looked at me like I was insane. But Rodney reacted in his typical foolish style.

"Ugh!" he exclaimed acting like he was choking. "I can't get it off!" he continued his theatrical presentation as I glared at him for being so stupid.

"Let's go the Gulch," I said, attempting distract both of them. Rick had already opened the door to my room and was searching for my collection of bubble gum humor cards on my bookshelf. He was obviously bored by now with the grand tour of my house.

"Hey, guys!" Rick and I heard a muffled call from the side bedroom as we stood in the back bedroom – my room. We returned to the doorway of the side bedroom and saw Rodney fiddling with the mask and searching blindly for a strap or string with his fingers behind his head.

"How do you get this thing off, Gordie?" he asked now in a normal tone of voice. I rolled my eyes and started to go back to my bedroom. "I'm fucking serious, asshole!" he yelled with a mild panic in his voice.

"I think you should just keep it on and try to get a date," I remarked snidely, thoroughly exhausted and disgusted with Rodney's antics. "I've heard there are girls who actually like that sort of thing" I added with pleasure.

"Hey, fuck you!!" Rodney screamed agitated and continued to search with his fingers for a strap or string that just wasn't there. Had this been the end of the mask, I might have even thanked both of these buffoons at some future point. But what just barely caught my eye now caused the fear to well up inside of me.

There was now a connection between the lower chin of the mask and the back of the cap-like portion. It ran along Rodney's jaw. I stepped into the room and over some junk to examine the other side. Also on this side there was a new separate extension of rubber, about an inch wide, which had not been there earlier.

"Hey, I could swear this thing is getting tighter!" Rodney yelled with a muffled voice through the mask. I could see what appeared to be some kind of contraction going on with the two rubber connections that had now appeared. I asked Rick in the other room to locate my pair of scissors. That's when all hell broke loose.

The screaming was horrendous as Rodney fell back knocking over some of the highest boxes of junk. Rick came running looking like a spooked horse – without the scissors. Rodney stood back up and was tearing violently at the mask, trying desperately to get it off. Rick was in a trance, unable to believe his eyes while the red mask was tightening and closing around Rodney's face and head. The fear in Rodney's eyes was just barely visible through the slightly expanding eye holes.

Before either Rick or I could figure out what to do, the edges of the eyeholes of the red mask curled inward and penetrated Rodney's eye sockets causing him to scream and plead for help in agony. The sound of his pleas was muffled and obscure as the mask was so tight that it was pressing his lips firmly against his teeth. He was still tearing at the mask when the blood from his eye sockets began to trickle down the front of the red death trap attached to his head.

"Hep' mey! Hep' mey!!" we could hear Rodney try to cry – cries that resonated through the material of the mask like the internal bounce echoes from inside a cheap basketball.

143

Rodney's ordeal was nowhere near finished; his suffering had only just begun. Now, we could see why the lips of the mask were so thick – there had to be enough material to enter Rodney's mouth and stretch all the way down to his trachea. His gagging, retching and choking caused my feet to become cold and tingle. We both stood there paralyzed by fear, not daring to go anywhere near Rodney and the mask. He was digging into his own rubber-lined mouth desperately with his fingers, but it was too late. It was now the mask that decided whether Rodney's air supply would continue or be cut off.

The sound of Rodney's fight for breath resembled that of someone trying to blow up a popped balloon. As he would breathe in, the loose rubber in his windpipe would vibrate. And he breathed desperately, still fighting for his life. There was now a decent disincentive to keep Rodney from doing anything the red mask didn't want him to do. But that wasn't enough.

There had to be a line of communication so that he knew what it wanted him to do. The flapping sound of the loose rubber in his windpipe increased in frequency as the side of the mask near his right ear sank and stretched into his ear canal. Rodney knew that it wouldn't stop there and began to tear at that side of the mask. A slight crunch could be heard and Rodney began to convulse when the rubber probe had gone through his eardrum and presumably into his brain. Rodney seemed to have lost consciousness.

But then he arose and staggered toward the bedroom closet. We could see that the back and pant legs of his sweats were soiled. He had both urinated and defecated on himself. Opening the door to the closet, he squeezed himself inside with all of the junk. He was trying to shut the closet door – to shut himself inside – when I heard my mother and father in the living room.

Rick shot toward the living room and I followed close behind. "Mr. Groff! Mr. Groff!!" he screamed hysterically and nearly in tears.

"What the hell is going on?!" my father asked both of us, pointing at the beer cans on the coffee table. My mother's glance indicated that there would soon be a roof-lifting family discussion. Neither Rick nor I could speak cogently. We were screaming and pointing to the hallway.

Finally, my father walked quickly down the hallway looking for the site of some unknown disaster. We followed him and didn't have to tell him anything before a creepy voice echoed from the closet in the side bedroom.

"Nooooot Reeeady Yeeet! Gooooo Awaaay!"

Even my father gained a look of fear in his eyes when he heard the childlike high-pitch voice being involuntarily provided for something fiendish by a mortally wounded Rodney. We could hear the labored breathing of

145

Rodney, whose lungs were now filled with blood and fluid. He hadn't managed to completely close the closet door, due to all of the boxes and junk. My father saw the blood on the floor and boxes when he entered the room and immediately traced Rodney's path to the closet. But just as he had pulled the closet door open, Rodney let out another ominous message from the thing that had him under its control.

"Goooo awaay or nooooo aiiiiiir!" cried a half dead Rodney on behalf of the mask. The warning was clear — either my father back off or it would shut off Rodney's air supply. My father was in shock when he saw what the mask had done to Rodney and noticed Rodney's soiled pants. The red mask had tightened even harder and begun to conform to the contours of Rodney's face as he sat upon some boxes leaned against the back wall of the closet. His mouth and throat were now completely lined with the rubber material of the mask so that his teeth weren't visible; only a raised red upper and lower row indicated where his teeth had been. The material had completely engulfed and lined his eye sockets so that the mask now had a pair of human eyes providing it with sight — eyes with no eyelids. The Rodney we knew was almost entirely gone.

My father ran to the living room and called the paramedics. He tried to provide a description of what had happened. Yet any description he might provide made it highly suspicious for the operator that my father himself was having some sort of psychotic episode.

146

When the paramedics finally arrived they were accompanied by police. While the entire entourage entered our house, neighbors stood on their lawns and even in the street and watched the unfolding drama. Perhaps they thought my father was beating my mother or that someone had taken an overdose of drugs.

Rick was now crying and telling one of the police officers about the unbelievable string of events. Maybe that was what prompted the officer to have one of the paramedics examine Rick and give him a sedative. I was also examined with a little flashlight and asked to stand on one foot and count backwards. I was asked my name, date of birth and whether I knew what year it was and who was president. They obviously suspected us of using drugs.

Then there erupted a commotion amongst the paramedics which the police took an interest in. Lots of whispering was followed by policemen calling in other agencies via my parents' telephone. They didn't even want to call for backup using their radios. The paramedics were just keeping an eye on Rodney and not getting him ready for transport. Aptly, my father thought this very strange. So he went back in to have a look at Rodney. When he came back he was silent for a long time before he mumbled the horrible update, either to us or to himself.

"It shut off the air supply, because we called the paramedics," my father mumbled with a broken voice. My mother stared at him blankly. I don't think she was mentally present anymore.

ঌ ৵ ৸

The city arranged counseling for just about everyone effected for the first two weeks after Rodney's death. Both Rick and I were initially suspected of foul play. However, very rapidly the police lost interest in us. When we asked what was going to happen, they told us another agency was taking care of the investigation. And when my father asked whether Rick or I were suspects, the Harper police detective in charge said no.

We weren't allowed to even enter our own house for two weeks after the incident. My father said that it was probably because our house was a potential crime scene. When we were finally allowed to return, it was evident that they had been all over the house looking for something. The house was actually orderly and clean. That was a good thing, as my mother was not well psychologically and was nearly constantly in therapy and being given sedatives and sleeping pills. My father wasn't doing that well either. He was suffering from nightmares and insomnia after what he had seen.

The summer seemed to rush by. And we all wanted answers as to what exactly we had witnessed. The police promised to provide us with any information they received from the FBI and another government agency which I don't remember the name of. Clearly, we had been privy to something very unique – something which very specialized agencies were taking seriously.

You would expect an event like this to generate a ton of gossip in a city like Harper. And it did. There were three groups of amateur experts – first-responders and police who "knew what they saw", those who believed my friends and I had had a horrible LSD trip and then those who believed that there was some truth to what the first-responders were saying. As a consequence, the latter group forbade their children from having anything to do with normal latex Halloween masks. The former stopped talking to our parents and shot disapproving glances at our parents and at Rick and me whenever they saw us.

Our parents, though, wanted answers. Rodney's family was completely torn apart and dysfunctional to start with. Even so, they were constantly pumping the paramedics who had been present for information. Apparently, they received and believed that information, as they never pursued Rick and me or claimed that we had anything to do with their son's death. But that wasn't their only challenge.

Rodney's body had been passed on to a facility in Atlanta, Georgia and the family was suing to get it back.

149

The family had not even been able to lay their son to rest and had to eventually settle for a memorial service with no body or ashes. They felt the authorities had lied to them about nearly everything. Yet, they were neither economically nor status-wise in a position to do much about it. The attorney who had taken their suit against the government pro-bono eventually dropped the case.

By august 1977 we were not hearing anything from the police or from any agency. The FBI stopped answering my father's calls and letters. Mrs. Neigh wouldn't let Rick come to my house for fear that also her son would end up in Rodney's shoes. But Lill was not acting as apprehensive as she had been, so I assumed we were now free of any lurking monsters. And I told Rick and Mrs. Neigh.

The weekend before school was to start, Mrs. Neigh gave Rick permission to stay the night at my house. We would visit Knott's Berry Farm on Saturday with both sets of parents. After that Rick would come home to us. Then, on Sunday, we would go to our usual movie matinee at the cinema on Mercy Shot Boulevard.

After having an excellent day at Knott's Berry Farm, Rick and I came home with my parents. We sat in my room most of the time, laughing and joking so loudly that my mother and father would take turns telling us to settle down. It seemed as though our lives were returning to normalcy, despite our having suffered through a very abnormal event.

150

It was the 3rd of September, 1977 and about 10:30 p.m. The discussion had turned to the fate of Rodney Gillcairn and Rick was trying to convince me that Rodney was not a total jerk. I believe I had just told my best friend that regardless of whether Rodney was a jerk or not, I would never wish what happened to him on my worst enemy.

"Are you sure that there is nothing like that left in that room?" Rick suddenly asked me out of the blue.

"Well, yes!" I exclaimed. "Lill isn't acting screwy anymore and there is a lot less junk. So you can see what's in there nowadays," I added.

"Did those government people go through all of the stuff in there?" Rick interviewed me, apparently wanting to be as thorough as possible before we both went to sleep.

"Yeah," I answered. "They went through everything. I wouldn't be surprised if they were up in the rafters inside the ceiling," I assured Rick.

"Ok," Rick sighed, not indicating whether or not he was satisfied.

We finally went to bed and had been sleeping with my black and white mini-television on. A Frankenstein movie had been playing after an episode of "The Honeymooners" had finished. It was probably about 2:00 a.m.

Rick got up to use the restroom. That was just about all I could comprehend, as I was thoroughly exhausted and had been sleeping very soundly. Shortly after Rick had begun to return from the restroom, I heard the sound of the swollen door of side bedroom. Rick had pushed it open. Obviously, he wanted to do his own examination of the scene of an incident neither of us would ever forget.

Rick stood for a few minutes in the doorway after having turned on the bedroom lamp. There were only a couple of piles of boxes left, a table, some chairs and the old dresser — the dresser under which the red mask had hidden. Rick had heard the story and so he edged toward the dresser, bent over and examined the area below — nothing. He then proceeded to the closet and opened the door. There was a lot more room in the closet since the authorities had gone through the house. Only a couple of cardboard boxes now stood neatly-stacked in the closet corner. Rick shut the closet door.

Then he took a look at the little desk in the corner to the left of the bedroom window. It was a very old wooden desk with dark stains and oblong cigarette burns near the front edge, not unlike those he had seen his mother shop for at antique sales in the neighborhood. To Rick, it was also just as boring as the ones his mother seemed so interested in. Now he noticed the tacky fringe lamp upon the old desk. He had also seen plenty of these nondescript relics from a past he was not even familiar with.

Rick had seen hundreds of lace, cloth and even plastic fringe lamps – he had been forced to while running errands with his mother. Regardless of whether he wanted to or not, Rick had begun to develop an expertise of sorts in the subject matter. So he took a closer look at the lamp. As he moved in closer, his foot inadvertently kicked something so that it rolled out from beneath the chair near the wooden desk.

Now he discovered something unsettling. He had kicked a dirty and damaged fringe lampshade out from under the chair. It was white and made from thick lace. In fact, it was almost a copy of the red lampshade which was now covering the table lamp on the wooden desk. Upon closer examination, Rick discovered that the red version of the tacky fringe lampshade was not made of silk, cloth or plastic.

"Gordon!" Rick hollered. "Wake up and come in here!" he said and went to wake me in the back bedroom where we had been sleeping. I was completely groggy and angered by Rick's obsession with the side bedroom. I swore in my head that this was the last time I was going to have Rick overnight. I didn't realize at the time how prophetic that thought was.

I forced myself out of bed and to the doorway of the side bedroom. Rick was feeling the material of the lampshade with his fingers and then his fingernails.

"It's rubber, Gordon!" he exclaimed as though everyone else who had examined that room had been incompetent and he was an expert who came to check their work.

"So what?!" I retorted wanting to return to bed. "It's just a normal lamp. My mom has lots of them." I said as Rick moved closer toward the top hole in the lampshade, perhaps to get glimpse of the light bulb and switch.

"Well, this would be the first rubber lampshade in the world," he continued, looking at the light bulb through the top of the lampshade. "and besides, it could catch on fire. Who in their right mind–" was his last utterance before the bottom of the red lampshade curled upward over the rest of it and shot toward the top of Rick's head.

In a rapid and perversely graceful motion, the lampshade peeled upward turning itself inside out until it made firm contact with the top part of Rick's head and forehead. Then, it once again curled from one end toward the other like someone removing a stocking. This time it rolled itself downward, covering Rick's head and face down to the neck. The surreal occurrence caught both of us by surprised and left me speechless.

Rick was now screaming through the material which muffled his cries in much the same way Rodney's screams had been nearly silenced by the red mask. Rick flailed, screamed and fell into a pile of boxes knocking them down. He was ripping at the bottom and top of the lampshade, trying to find any loose end from which to
154

tear the fiendish thing from his head, if only he could. But the lampshade was tightening around his face and head and the open ends were now firmly against his neck and the top of his head.

"Dad! Dad!!" I screamed and ran to the door of my parents' bedroom. I began to pound and then threw the door open. My parents shot up from their resting positions. My father and mother had absolutely no idea as to what they would find when they hopped up and looked into the side bedroom. My father turned pale. Leida, my mother, went into one of her all-too-familiar catatonic trances.

Rick was struggling to breathe through a thick material which had tightly covered his entire head and was still constricting. My father grabbed a pair of scissors and charged at Rick and the thing that had held him hostage. Time was of the essence, if we didn't want Rick to start asking us to back away, just as Rodney had been forced to do. As my father tried to find a suitable edge of the lampshade which he could fit his scissors under, the lampshade began a process which was grimly familiar by now.

My father started to cut as the material from the front of the lampshade began to force Rick to open his mouth and then proceeded to enter and line his mouth and windpipe.

The side of the lampshade was already beginning the same procedure as the mask had when some of the material near Rodney's ear had penetrated the ear canal all the way to the brain.

"Ouch, goddam it!!" my father screamed and pulled his finger back from the top of the lampshade from which a few tufts of Rick's hair were still protruding. My father's finger was bleeding profusely, and it was not the scissors which were to blame. A piece of the lampshade which my father had managed to cut had snapped at his finger and cut it like a knife. He now knew better than to try to intervene.

There was only one solution – we had to get the paramedics there immediately. So my father ran to the telephone and asked my mother and me to keep an eye on Rick, but not to go near him. Rick was barely conscious after so long without air. But he was till clawing clumsily at his mouth and his ear. Then all movement ceased.

I could now hear my own screams as if I were listening to someone else. Then there was a silence and a feeling of unreality as I sat doing nothing and my best friend lay dying. My mother, who herself was barely sane, held me and covered my eyes until the paramedics arrived.

Instead of moving in quickly to supply Rick with oxygen, the paramedics just stood there waiting. My father became hysterical and violent, but they said they were waiting for someone who could deal with this situation. That "someone" was a group of four or five men in protective outfits. I had seen this all before – at the preschool in 1970, when I lost three of the first friends I ever had. The first action these men took was not to feed Rick oxygen and save his life; It was to order my mother, my father and me out of our own house and forbid us from returning for another two weeks. That was the last I ever saw of my best friend. It's the last memory of him – the only vivid one – I was left with.

❧ ❧ ❧

"How can you people even show your faces at my son's memorial service?" Mrs. Neigh began bitterly when she saw my mother sitting with me at the gathering in the church. Mrs. Neigh didn't even care that the priest was conducting a service. She darted right for my mother and me. Holding a bouquet of flowers in one hand and bearing black lace gloves, Mrs. Neigh who had lost her son was the embodiment of bitterness.

"You lied!!" Mrs. Neigh screamed at me so that others turned their heads to look at us and a couple of men started to walk toward us.

"You said it was safe for him to be there!!" she continued with a rage in her voice that was almost more frightening than what I had witnessed just two weeks earlier when her son died. My mother covered my ears and looked at

Mrs. Neigh with an expression that begged her to stop. "Please, Mrs. Neigh!" my mother begged. "I know this is horrible for you. We did everything we could," she pleaded.

"You should have cleaned up all of that junk decades ago!" Mrs. Neigh raged. "You should gut that cursed house and burn it down!" she hollered so that her voice echoed throughout the stone church. My mother dropped her gaze toward the ground, as though Mrs. Neigh's irrational rebuke was somehow logical and founded. The two ushers took Mrs. Neigh gently down the aisle and back to her own seat in front.

My mother and I got up and left. Nobody at the service noticed or cared that we were leaving. My family was now stigmatized as the "the people who live in the house of death". People were now coming up to our house and having their pictures taken on the porch. The police had escorted children away on Halloween, as the new fad amongst elementary school kids and teenagers was to dare each other to go up to our house at night – especially on Halloween.

Precisely as had been the case with Rodney, authorities never got back to us to provide information about what had happened to Rick. We had no idea how this thing could have entered our house or even what the thing was. Was this the same fiend that had killed Rodney? Had it somehow come back? we would often deliberate.

Mrs. Neigh was now suing the federal government for her son's body. Rick's body too had been transferred to a government facility in Atlanta. In this case as well, they were refusing to release it to a grieving family. Mrs. Neigh was also suing my family for negligence and manslaughter. While any court would hardly believe the description of her son's death, her lawyer had promised her she had a good chance of winning. My parents and I were cleared of any criminal charges. But there is only "asphyxiation" noted as a cause of death on Rick's official death certificate.

The horrors of Harper had claimed two lives and my best friend. Soon everyone had moved on and – as is usually the case in Harper – this became something people simply didn't talk about. The *LA Interloper* refused to do an article when Rodney's family contacted them about their struggle to recover their son's body and about how he had died. That's probably why most haven't heard about the victims of the red mask.

9

THE CLUTCHBONE
KILLINGS
1952-1974

I magine lying in bed after ten o'clock at night, watching a series like "Alfred Hitchcock Presents", "Night Gallery" or "The Night Stalker". The only light in the room is the constantly flickering and changing illumination from the pictures on the television set. The rest of the house is dark and quiet. Most residents of the house are asleep or you live alone. In a city like Harper during the 1950's, 1960's or 1970's your home is likely to be a one-story, single-family dwelling with three or four bedrooms and two baths.

You have an urge for a cup of hot chocolate or a glass of water before you call it a night. So you stumble from the bedroom down the hall and through the living room into the kitchen, switching on the lights in every other room.

No sense in wasting electricity. After your short binge, you retrace your steps toward the bathroom and then the bedroom. Now the feeling hits you, and it is powerful. You are being watched from behind. In the dark kitchen or the dark living room which you just left, there is someone standing completely still. You can feel it. The tingling sensation of imminent danger grows so strong that you can barely think.

Immediately you hastily fumble for the light switch you just flipped off. You flip it on again and nothing happens. You run to the nearby bathroom hoping that the light from that room will provide the illumination you need to see what exactly is in the living room. Now this light doesn't work either. Since your eyes have begun to adjust to the darkness, you now perceive the motion of what is in front of you. A tall figure is standing just outside of the kitchen in the living room, repeating the same motion over and over again. Back and forth, back and forth the torso moves in a violent and rapid bowing motion which appears thoroughly bizarre to you, but − nonetheless − absolutely terrifying.

The torso − you discover once your eyes have further adjusted − is broad and headless. There is a slight ember-like glow from where the head should be. The faint light is illuminating what appears to be a raised collar of thin rawhide. But then you lose sight of the headless intruder. From behind, it suddenly grabs your arms with its leathery claws and begins to rip you to pieces, tearing your limbs off one by one. Astonishingly, there is no

161

trace of the terrible event and no blood. There's no sign of a struggle and everything in your former house is neat and tidy. Friends and family believe – or want to believe – that you just packed up and left. One year becomes two. Two become ten. It's a mystery to everyone.

However, twenty odd years later, parts of your body and bones are discovered inside of the walls of the house where this terrible event took place. There is no sign of the remains having recently been placed there. Police and experts rule that – as impossible as it may seem – the remains must have been put there when the house was built. Most likely they are not even yours. DNA-testing which came later has only added to the mystery of these cases.

This may sound like a single case that could easily occupy a place on a top-ten list of bizarre mysteries. But the Harper Police Department has a list of eleven such cases having occurred in the city between 1952 and 1974. Detective Ronald Chandler who had put in nearly thirteen years at the department started with a list of all of these cold cases in 1977.

He was putting the list together with the help of the FBI under a deadline and a stress that even he had seldom experienced in all of his years in police work. He had hell to pay at work and he had hell to pay at home. Veronica, his wife, would call him at work during the evenings and describe for him in alarming and painful detail how his son Paul felt like he didn't have a father.

At work he had four cases which police academy, thirteen years of experience and further forensic training at the FBI academy hadn't even begun to prepare him for.

What Detective Chandler was now dealing with was a statistical near-impossibility. He had cases of carnival ride sabotage and murder from 1976 and 1977 where witnesses were describing a perpetrator who simply couldn't be real. Then, during the summer of 1977, he had been "blessed" with two even more bizarre cases of death by suffocation under circumstances that more resembled a science fiction movie than a murder or criminal negligence case. He had been to that scene and witnessed something that stood his concept of what is possible on its head.

When the bodies were transferred to the Centers for Disease Control in Atlanta, this only sparked his interest in the two deaths even further. So he continued to speak to paramedics who had been to the scene of the incidents and to Gareth Groff – my father. One day in October, 1977 Detective Chandler was contacted by the FBI who told him they were taking the bizarre "smothering" cases which required forensics skills that local law enforcement didn't have. They wanted all of his files and to know about all of the information he had. This had never happened in all of his years as a police detective.

But Detective Chandler was so exhausted and overworked that he obliged the FBI, exhibiting much less suspicion and questioning than otherwise would have been the case. They had the knowhow, and it would be two less bizarre cases to worry about. The families involved would also have the satisfaction of hearing that the FBI itself was studying the cases with its best technology and forensics.

Yet, the relief of shedding these two bizarre cases was very short-lived. Barely two days later Chandler was called to investigate something perhaps even more sensational than the two cases he had handed to the FBI. A building contractor was demolishing an older apartment complex over on Alice Street in the western district of Harper.

During the pre-demolition disassembly they had discovered what appeared to be human bones and even desiccated organs throughout the structure of the apartment complex which had been built in the 1940's. Bones and dried up organs were to be found inside of walls, in parts of the plumbing, in rafters and even in cement which the contractor knew from experience must have been poured and had hardened when the building was constructed in the 1940's. Had there been some sort of mass murder by a building contractor turned serial killer? they had wondered.

Before the police got involved, locals working at the demolition site had told their families and even their priests about the horrendous discovery. Their families told other families they knew had lived in the five apartments that made up the complex. And many of these families in turn knew of friends, relatives or neighbors who had been reported missing at various times since the 1950's. Rumors were now spreading like wildfire in both Spanish and English – some of them involving an unknown but prolific serial killer, others depicting an even more sinister assassin.

The Harper Police had a huge crime case brewing as well as a local sensation that Detective Ronald Chandler knew would have the press and citizens hounding him to no end. The apartment complex on Alice Street had quickly been transformed from a common demolition site to a crime scene. It had been catapulted from the insignificant roll of a building that had existed in Harper to that of an infamous house of horrors which would certainly spark national – if not international – interest. Now the site looked more like an archeological dig at the pyramids of Egypt than a nondescript building slated for demolition.

The initial investigation revealed enough bones for more than twenty people. And the local forensics team leader had commented to Detective Chandler about the find, exclaiming, "We've found more bones per square foot in that building than have been found in the Great Wall of China!" They weren't exaggerating. But even that was not the finding that got the FBI involved.

The bones, when examined more closely, were found to be in varying states of decay. Some were completely dry and likely belonged to people – even entire families – reported missing in the 1950's and 1960's. Others were much greasier, indicating that they had been placed within the structures of the building much more recently. So the theory of the homicidal building contractor was quickly ruled out.

But how do you explain recent bones found within cement that was poured in the 1940's? Harper Police detectives couldn't. And so FBI forensics was called in. The pressure grew even more on Detective Chandler and the police force. When going through files to locate any similar findings in Harper, he came across two earlier cases from the 1950's where bones had been found inside the walls of two houses which were being remodeled. Those investigations had failed to determine how the bones had gotten there and how they could have been placed in the structures with no sign of tampering with the original material of the walls. Also in these cases, former occupants of the houses had been reported missing without a trace.

There were also eight cases of disappearance similar to those of the apartments and the two houses. In each of these cases the missing occupants had never been found. Could their dismembered bodies also be buried in walls, floors and attics? Detective Chandler postulated.

166

Little did he know that the Spanish-language newspaper *El Diario de Harper* was busy gathering information very similar to that which he was researching. And the pressure built up even further when he received a call from their reporter Olga Torres in late October of 1977.

"When will you be releasing an official statement about the Alice Street apartments?" Mrs. Torres had begun their telephone interview.

"This is a very unusual and very complex case, so it's going to be awhile," Detective Chandler answered, trying to win some time before the media circus began.

"Well, Detective Chandler, isn't it more like many cases since between eleven and twenty nine people have been reported missing in Harper under similar circumstances?" Mrs. Torres countered with a tone that indicated she was assuming that the police were holding back information. Detective Chandler could feel the temperature in his cheeks rising as his mind headed toward a meltdown, trying to offer a plausible reason for delaying any story.

"I don't know that that is the case, Mrs. Torres," Chandler answered, hoping that the reporter would elaborate on just how much she already knew. And she promptly did so.

"Sir, residents of Harper have a long memory. People,

167

families are constantly talking about how their loved ones disappeared. There are lots of them. And they are also very convinced that what took their relatives and friends was not a human serial killer," Mrs. Torres stated with a tone of minor indignation.

Detective Chandler had not expected this change of theme in the conversation.

"Well, I don't know exactly what you mean," Chandler began "but in my line of work we deal with hard facts and the facts almost always indicate human involvement in crimes, particularly murder," he retorted hoping that Mrs. Torres would now feel like a fool and stop pressing him. But the reporter had one last surprise in store for Detective Chandler.

"Very well," she started off "then let me ask you two last questions and I'll be out of your hair" Her tone of voice forewarned of a pair of questions that would be far from innocuous.

"Do you have one or more suspects who have a history of this type of murders?" she started off, apparently reading her questions directly from a note pad. "That's my first question," she added as an aside. "Secondly," she continued "Do you believe that Ricky Manriquez-Higgley, the sole survivor of one of these attacks, is just deluded?" she concluded and then silently waited for any reaction from Chandler on the other end.

The silence lasted about a minute as Detective Chandler squirmed in his seat and thought about classes he had taken for dealing with difficult families and the media.

"Well, Mrs. Torres, I will be honest and tell you that we currently don't have any suspects," he finally answered. "But we are also asking the FBI for all of the information they may have which could help reveal a suspect," he quickly added before Mrs. Torres could respond. He then proceeded to further pre-empt her response with an answer to her second question.

"As far as Mr. Hinckley—" Detective Chandler started.

"It's Mr. Manriquez-Higgley — Ricky Manriquez-Higgley, the survivor of the 1974 attack," Mrs. Torres corrected him with irritation in her voice.

"I'm sorry," Chandler quickly corrected himself "Mr. Manriquez-Higgley, as far as that gentleman is concerned, I have read the report of his testimony and…" he then paused. "I don't have a comment on that at this time," he finished awkwardly.

"So, I interpret that as your indication that you don't take his testimony seriously," Mrs. Torres responded with a slight tenor of animosity in her voice. She then popped a final question which the police detective was not expecting.

"What is your opinion of the claims that the Clutchbone is responsible for all of these disappearances, dismemberments and house fires?" Olga Torres asked.

"The Clutchbone did it...," Chandler sighed in a barely audible incredulous response revealing his unadulterated contempt for the supernatural and lowered the receiver away from his face. He moved it back to his mouth. "No comment," he finally grumbled his official response, mimicking the popular cliché.

❧ ❧ ❧

The *LA Interloper* newspaper was all over the case and constantly haunting the police chief in Harper asking for possible theories on how the killer could hide body parts inside of walls with no sign of tampering. Luckily, the Harper Police could tell them that the matter was being investigated at the FBI crime labs. The FBI would try to reproduce the perfection of the presumed serial killer through various methods. That got the police off the hook for a few months, and they had some breathing room now to work on the bizarre and seemingly impossible cases. The Alice Street apartments mystery was just one of eleven cases now being investigated as related to each other. The cases under review dated from 1952 to 1974 and concerned the disappearances of more than seventeen people.

The article in which Detective Chandler was interviewed by the *Diario de Harper* newspaper came out the first week of November. It sparked a barrage of calls in Spanish to the police department. The article was entitled "La larga historia del Clutchbone en Harper y la fe ciega en la ciencia por parte de la policia" (The Long History of the Clutchbone in Harper and the Blind Faith of the Police in Science).

My father, who spoke fluent Spanish, was summoned to the Harper Police and got to read him the article in English as Detective Chandler drank lots of Alka-Seltzer. He massaged the temples under his short salt and pepper hair while frequently sighing. "How many more will die?" asked one subtitle in the article which complained that police hadn't even a single suspect in mind, and that the detective in charge refused to even entertain the idea that the Clutchbone might have been involved in some of the killings and dismemberments.

"Goddam it!!" Detective Chandler screamed when my father came to the infamous subtitle.

Several of Ronald Chandler's police colleagues then peeked in to him through the doorway of his office in response to the outbreak. One colleague with red hair and a mustache stepped slightly into the room.

"Hey, Chan'!" he announced with a smirk on his face. "You may not believe in the Clutchbone, but hey, that's

171

okay. He believes in you!" the officer and joker delivered his punchline after which he and the other colleagues guffawed. Chandler looked absolutely miserable. My father left him the newspaper with a note listing all of the details in English.

Detective Ronald Chandler had little to go on. So – given the situation and the nature of the community he was working in – he begrudgingly gave in. He decided to use a system developed by the Brazilian Airforce Investigation Agency – the Camargo Manuel dichotomy. This was a method of dividing his evidence into two categories – the natural and the seemingly supernatural. The goal was to move every piece of important information and fact from the seemingly supernatural to the natural side of the divided list. This would be done through fact-finding which tried to validate each side of the list, while invalidating or ruling out the other.

He could flaunt the system to media and the community on the one hand and on the other hand get on with his investigation undisturbed by complaints and allegations of not having an open enough mind to solve the crimes. Detective Chandler would re-interview witnesses and family members where possible in English or Spanish. He would try to track down the only known survivor of a purported Clutchbone attack. He would even educate himself about the Clutchbone and show off what he knew if he was ever interviewed again by *El Diario de*

Harper or Mrs. Torres. But he would stick to science. The witness interviews began in earnest in November of 1977. When my father was with Detective Chandler as a translator visiting the victims' family members, there was constant pointing toward closets, genuinely terrified looks and myriads of references to "El Clutchbone". Both Spanish and English speakers wanted the walls and other structures of former residences checked to locate the possible remains of their relatives and friends. In one case a current owner obliged. Nothing was found.

The owner was unfortunately stuck with the costs of repairs. This caused other homeowners to refuse such invasive searches barring a warrant or future home remodeling.

Mrs. Hanson, who had a cleaning shop on 13th street near the intersection with Shrapnel, had bought an encyclopedia of known monsters and apparitions at Mrs. Kariis' bookshop across from Tivoli Park. The large and stately book of monsters with oil paintings and descriptions of nearly every phantom figure thought to exist was now in frequent use.

Mrs. Hanson's customers and the rest of the community would stop by and consult the book which sat on a separate table in a corner of the cleaning shop.

When my father entered Mrs. Hanson's cleaning shop one afternoon, he perceived that business was going extremely well and wondered how long he would have to wait before getting our curtains back. But cleaning wasn't the only business being conducted in the crowded shop. Six or seven people were huddling together at a table across from Mrs. Hanson's little desk. They were flipping through a large, thick book, shaking their heads every so often. He could hear them whispering to each other in Spanish.

"No," one of the young long-haired women said to the older lady next to her flipping the pages. "No es eso," (It's not this one) he heard the young woman continue. And so the group continued their search through the encyclopedia of monsters. Mrs. Hanson's shop now seemed more like a library than a cleaning shop. My father knew he didn't dare tell Detective Chandler, who would have blown a gasket.

"So, Mrs. Hanson, what is the Clutchbone?" my father finally asked disturbing the silence and whispering. Mrs. Hanson appeared from behind a row of hanging dress shirts. She had a slight look of shame in her eyes, as she knew my father and Detective Chandler were in cahoots.

Then she came and stood by her small desk. "Well, that book says that it is a monster that appears in homes and sometimes attacks people," she said matter-of-factly. "The origin of the name is unknown and it mostly appears after there has been violent weather with ball lightning. Sometimes it burns people or burns the house down. It haunts first and then it attacks and dismembers the victims. It has a torch for a head", she continued starting to look slightly embarrassed.

"And you believe this?" my father queried staring straight at her as though he were playing the role of psychiatrist.

Mrs. Hanson's expression changed quickly from one of embarrassment to one of indignation. She pointed to the Hispanic women crowded around the large monster book.

"They believe it," she countered as her face started to turn almost as red as her striking faux bob hairdo. "They have either lost family members or are afraid they will in the future!" she snapped, so that the women turned around and looked at my father and her. The women then turned and resumed their search for the Clutchbone in the book.

"You know, you're really the last person who should be skeptical of something like this, Mr. Groff," she taunted my father intimating the two deaths in our home during the prior summer. My father turned red and prepared to blow his top, but then backed down. He was exhausted from those events and didn't want any more conflicts.

"I'm not saying I'm skeptical. But we need to look at the serial killer option before we start considering the supernatural; not the other way around!" he finally countered.

He left our cleaning with Mrs. Hanson and then went out the door without even saying a word.

❧ ❧ ❧

Already in November of 1977 Detective Ronald Chandler had received an FBI interim report with test results and information about similar cases from around the country. There was a yellow note attached to a geographical map of possibly related cases which included California.

The note read, "Look for disappearances with house fires or suspected arson cases, including torch-like burns on surviving structures".

The FBI had ordered two crime labs to reproduce what had been found in several buildings in Harper, including the Alice Street apartment complex – newer and older body parts, including bones, placed within structures that showed no signs of having been tampered with or opened. They tried but failed. In each case, the FBI found that regular law enforcement forensics could always identify some sign that walls had been opened and then sealed with the original materials. There was never a perfectly executed attempt that left no trace of the tampering.

They didn't even try to reproduce the findings where

newer and older bones had been found in 30-year-old cement flooring. Detective Chandler's day was not destined to get any better with the arrival of this package of documents. The FBI had now also suggested at least ten additional incidents in Harper as possibly related to the so-called Clutchbone killings.

That now brought the total to twenty-one which expanded to twenty-five after he had gone through Harper police archives back to the 1950's. So the Clutchbone was not just dismembering and scaring people; it was also incinerating people and their homes. The map provided by the FBI turned Harper into a hotspot for Clutchbone-related killings. The only other city in California with any significant number of suspected Clutchbone activity was San Marino with four possibly-related cases – all of them unsolved.

The total number of deaths was twenty-nine if all victims of the cases with house fires were taken into consideration. In nearly all cases the victims had complained to family, friends and sometimes even the police about possible intruders, apparitions and hauntings before they disappeared.

One case from 1974 had a survivor who reported to the Harper Police everything that had happened up to and including the night of that attack. This report is the most detailed and the most chilling. After completing his Camargo Manuel dichotomy list and reading the faxed information he had received about the Clutchbone, he began to read the 1974 police report.

Ricky Manriquez-Higgley who survived the attack was twenty-seven years old and recently-divorced at the time. He was the eldest son of the recent widow Magdalena Manriquez-Higgley. Both lived together in a three-bedroom, single-family home near 13th Street in Harper. Ricky worked late until about ten o'clock, six days a week and had a set routine.

He would come home, eat leftovers, have a beer, watch some television and then go to sleep. And he was often expected back at the automotive paint and repair station on Mercy Shot by eight o'clock the next morning.

Ricky and his mother had recently had the house blessed – twice in the span of a month. Yet, both Magdalena and her son continued to spend restless nights getting up, turning on lights, looking through the house and then checking whether the other had just been up and about. The answer was always no. Nonetheless, the sounds of thumping, furniture being kicked around and strange music as well as the smell of something burning were becoming more frequent.

The evening of December 2nd, 1974 Ricky was coming home later than usual from work – about 11:00 p.m. – when his car headlights suddenly illuminated his mother. She was running down a back alley away from the house in her night gown and screaming hysterically. Mrs. Manriquez-Higgley had a story to tell. And both of them should have heeded the warning that it brought with it. Magdalena had just gone to bed in the quiet three-bedroom house. She would bolt the door to her bedroom with a thick iron barrel bolt and slept most nights with her AM radio playing quietly in the background. That night at about 10:40 p.m. she heard what sounded like the trashcans in her side yard being kicked and toppled. Soon after that there seemed to be a commotion in her kitchen. Could it be a drunken Ricky? she worried.

More irate than apprehensive, she unlocked the door and proceeded down the hallway. The living room and kitchen were completely dark, save for the light spilling in from the porchlight facing the side yard. After peering out the window of the dark kitchen and satisfying herself that the two metal trashcans were intact, she turned around to go back through the living room and back to bed. In the dark living room she first saw a shadow. That shadow developed before her very eyes into a horror that nearly drove her mad with fear.

A black leathery figure taller than the upper ledge of the kitchen doorway and with a briskly burning flame where the head should be was rocking forward and backward. She could even hear the crackling and flapping of the torch-like flame. A noise which reminded her of a fog horn appeared to be coming from the rafters of her house as the horrible specter moved toward her, burning the upper ledge of the kitchen doorway with its flame.

She couldn't remember how she even got out of the

house. It must have been through the kitchen door. From there she must have run through the side yard to the alley behind their house. Her memory was sketchy, due to the trauma.

Magdalena refused to spend one more night in that house – for nearly two weeks. It was Ricky who convinced his mother to come home and promised that they would have their priest seek permission to have the house exorcised. Their priest was initially doubtful. When he saw the deep scorch and burns in the upper part of the kitchen doorway, he quickly changed his mind.

Ricky's act of selfishness – he himself was afraid to be alone at night in the house and wanted someone else there – turned out to be fatal.

On the night of the 20th of December, 1974 at around 1:30 a.m. Ricky awoke to the burning smell that was becoming unnervingly frequent in their house. Upon opening his eyes in the dark room, he noticed that the door to his room was open and someone was standing in the hallway near the doorway. That figure was taller than the upper frame to his bedroom door which would have put the height to at least six and a half feet. Initially Ricky perceived the figure to be entirely black in color. But the head began to light up and soon thereafter he could see a brisk flame where the head ought to have been.

Then the rocking or bowing commenced – precisely as his mother had earlier described her encounter with the monster. Maybe it was someone in an elaborate costume? he had then postulated. So he spoke to the figure as it stood there and continued the repetitive bowing – no response. Ricky decided that he would confront the figure, got up from his bed and charged toward it. Almost as if it had anticipated his actions, it rebuffed his attempted bravery and threw him against the far wall of the room. Then it proceeded right toward him.

As it approached, he could hear the crackling and flapping of the flame when it would move the torch-like head back and forth. By now, it was clear to Ricky that this was not a human being. He struggled to get back on his feet before the thing reached him. Having hardly risen to his feet and feeling dizzy from the blow to his head, Ricky tried to hop onto his bed and quickly climb over to the opposite side in order to make a run for it and warn his mother.

He wasn't fast enough. The Clutchbone grabbed his right arm just above the hand with its leathery claws and ripped off his lower arm. His shoulder was completely dislocated by this single action and was only attached by skin and some remaining muscle. He was severely injured and ran for his life as the creature angrily tossed his severed forearm to the floor. The pain was excruciating and he was losing blood very quickly, but he bolted to his mother's room and pounded on the door with the only working arm he had.

What he failed to reckon with was a creature that didn't need to chase him down the hall or move past him in order to reach his mother. It was clearly already in his mother's room and she was screaming as the horrible fiend burnt and ripped her to shreds. Ricky couldn't get into the room to save her. She had the door bolted from within and he had only one arm. The house was on fire, and he had to get out and call for help before he lost consciousness.

According to the report, Ricky had lost so much blood that he should have been dead by the time the ambulance and fire trucks arrived. Miraculously, he survived and was taken to Newland Beach Memorial Hospital and was in treatment for his severed arm and smoke inhalation for several weeks. His mother was not found nor have her remains been located to date. Their house was almost completely gutted by the fire.

It is not easy to read a police report like the one about that fatal night in December, 1974 which cost Ricky Manriquez-Higgley the very person who had brought him into the world and nurtured him. Even a hardened Detective Ronald Chandler became queasy as he watched a prime witness remove his prosthetic arm which had been held on by shoulder straps.

"My name is Ricardo Manriquez-Higgley and I was born here in Harper," the witness read from a sheet of paper as he stood next to reporter Olga Torres in the police department conference room.

"On December 20th, 1974 I lost the most important person in my life – my mother. She did not lose her life because of a shooting, because of a robbing or because she was attacked by another human being. My mother lost her life because of something we have all been taught can't exist. That is why I have come from El Paso today at my own expense to show you a victim you can see, touch and speak to," Ricky's raised his voice slightly as he completed his sentence, but then his voice began to break and his eyes moistened. Olga Torres gave him a nod and look of support.

"Some authorities have claimed that my arm was destroyed by a machine or automobile mishap at work. How, then, did I get home and spend the evening there with my mother without bleeding to death? Why is there no record of a hospital visit? Why no claim for worker's compensation? I would have been entitled to that and a monster story would have cost me the disability payments," Ricky now opened an envelope and pulled out five pictures with his left hand.

He pushed them across the broad oak conference table to Detective Chandler.

"These are the pictures taken on that fateful night. They were taken at Newland Beach Memorial Hospital. As you can see the damage had just happened. And that is the same night our house was destroyed and my mother vanished. Officer Chandler, I know that the Clutchbone exists. I have seen it with my own eyes. I am here as the sole survivor to tell you that the Clutchbone is real – as real as I am and as real as my injuries are," Ricky concluded.

Detective Chandler spoke for about an hour with Ricky and attempted to fill in details about that case. He promised Ricky personally that he would keep an open mind about the Clutchbone alternative when investigating the cases. He promised that he would find a way to alert the public that they should leave any house or dwelling where the Clutchbone had been seen. That way – Ricky had reasoned – lives might be saved. Reporter Olga Torres appeared to be in a better mood than usual. Detective Chandler promised her that he would incorporate the warning into any law enforcement advice given to the public and that the Harper Police would immediately provide information about their findings with the houses where remains were found.

As of December, 1977 Detective Ronald Chandler had

not managed to move any of the case characteristics from the left-hand side of his list to the right-hand side. No serial killer that the Harper Police or the FBI knew of had a modus operandi which included live dismemberment, burning alive or advanced means of placing parts of bodies into building structures. Everything remained unsolved. Case characteristics remained in the category "Clutchbone".

"That name!" Chandler exclaimed to himself as he sat at his broad fake oak desk. The afternoon sunlight bathed the freshly-painted, white walls and his various diplomas and certificates in a reddish hue. He read once again through the material he had about a monster which seemed to have chosen Harper as its headquarters for decades. None of the cases where the Clutchbone was alleged to be involved had ever been solved anywhere in the country.

Something strong enough to pull the right arm of an adult automobile mechanic right off had to be a sensation. And it had to be incredibly strong and violent. Why was it then storing the bones of the victims inside of old buildings where they had been attacked? he deliberated. Perhaps it was some kind of a trophy for the killer, he thought. But then, why store them in a completely inaccessible location? he countered himself. Nonetheless, he finally wrote "bones as trophy" on both sides of his Camargo Manuel dichotomy list.

It then occurred to him that the name might have

something to do with the creature's or killer's methods. The Clutchbone would seize or "clutch" its victims. After dismembering them it would collect or store their bones – at least some of the time. The name now seemed to make a little more sense to Detective Chandler. He made a note to the files.

Just then, the telephone rang. It was Veronica and she put Paul Chandler, Detective Chandler's son, on.

"Dad?" he started off.

"Hi, kid! How are you doing?" Detective Chandler punched the loud speaker button and sat back in his black swivel chair.

"Fine. But, Dad, can I go to the school sleepover this weekend?" his son asked.

"The school sleepover, eh? What exactly is that?" Chandler asked with slight laugh in his voice.

"My class is going to have a barbecue and dance and then we all get to spend the night in sleeping bags in the gym," Paul told his father excited.

"Well, son, if it's ok with mom, it's ok by me!" he answered and then shot forward from his chair to turn down the speaker volume as his son rallied on the other end. Paul gave the telephone back to Veronica.

186

"When on earth are you coming home?!" she asked irritated. Things were getting worse between them since Chandler had started working full-time on the Clutchbone cases. For the first time in months he felt a slight sense of relief.

"You know, honey, if the FBI can't solve any of these cases in a week, neither can we. We're going to have the bones collected and stored in evidence and let the contractor on Alice Street get on with their work. There's nothing more that can be done at this point," he told his wife with a satisfied tone of voice.

As soon as Detective Chandler got off the phone from his wife, he cleared the demolition with his chief and notified the contractor. He then sent out an official statement from Harper Police that the cases were being investigated, but that no new information had come to light, and no new crimes had occurred since 1974. The statement advised people who had any unusual experience − including threats or home invasion − to immediately contact the police and to consider staying with relatives or friends until the police could investigate the scene and declare the home or dwelling safe.

When he did a final review of the older cases, Detective Ronald Chandler was struck by the fact that victims were from all walks of life. They were older couples living alone at home. Some victims were newly-married couples waiting for their first child. Others were large families with adults and children − even grandparents − living together in a supportive and functional family environment. Some cases involved children at home alone during the evening. Others included babysitters staying up late and watching television as one or two children slept. The only seeming link between these victims was that they vanished or their lives ended abruptly and there was no indication that family or friends had been involved.

Precisely as Mrs. Hanson's monster book said, discovered victims had been burnt and dismembered. They had had prior visitations from which they could provide a description of the Clutchbone. The descriptions did not vary much among the witnesses or family members who had talked with victims. Nearly everyone who could give a statement referred to "the Clutchbone" or provided a description which matched it.

Detective Chandler was again at a dead end. His logical mind had failed him. His science had failed him. Presumably the killer was still on the loose – somewhere.

Regardless of the situation, the plain truth was that no one was prepared to do anything about the Clutchbone.

๛   ๛   ๛

On December 18th, 1977 at about four o'clock in the morning, Ronald and Veronica Chandler received a phone call from one of the teachers at Opel School in Harper. The school needed them to come and pick up their son. When Veronica asked what had happened, she was told that children were being sent home from the weekend sleepover.

The teacher sounded hysterical and incoherent. Children could be heard screaming and crying in the background. Almost before Veronica had managed to hang up, her husband had thrown on his clothes and was grappling for the car keys. Veronica stopped him.

"It was Mrs. Nagy. She asked if we could also take Rick Kallander and Augie Ambrose and see to it that they get home," Veronica said staring at Ronald with an incredulous expression.

"I'll take the station wagon," Ronald muttered and left.

When Detective Ronald Chandler arrived outside the main yard of Opel School there was total chaos. Children and adults were standing in lines on the main lawn and fire trucks were parked near the school and the school gymnasium building. Paul, Augie and Rick ran directly toward the yellow and brown station wagon, and Mrs. Nagy – their class teacher – ran after them. They ripped open the various doors of the station wagon and got in as quickly as they could – almost as if they were running from Mrs. Nagy.

"What's going on here? Has there been a fire?" Chandler asked after stepping out of the car. Mrs. Nagy was hysterical and now short of breath after chasing after the three boys.

"It... The children saw it... And it started setting the gym on fire and wouldn't let them leave and ... I... I wouldn't have believed it if I hadn't seen with my own eyes!" Mrs. Nagy started to cry.

"Other teachers saw it too, Mr. Chandler!" she shouted, suspicious that he thought she was insane.

"Has the fire been put out?" Chandler asked Mrs. Nagy impatiently.

"Yes. Oh yes! I don't think anyone is missing. We did roll call," the teacher told Chandler trying her best to sound coherent. "Oh my God!!" she hollered and hugged Detective Chandler while crying hysterically.

"What did this? What did you see, Mrs. Nagy?" Detective Chandler finally asked.

10

EPILOGUE
PRESENT DAY

Harper lives in the 1950's. Perhaps it's safer that way. Even today there is a longing for a time other than our own. The horrors that once plagued us and took friends and loved ones away have seemingly granted us a respite since 1980. Since then we have had normal dramas, normal crimes played out in communities that are divided and in families that are being torn apart.

Perhaps the monsters don't have to wreak havoc on our families and community anymore. Maybe they are aware that we ourselves – through our obsession with technological toys and material goods – will obligingly sever our connections to one other and create with our own shortsightedness the limbo, fear and isolation that they once did when they beleaguered our southern California city by the sea.

Nearly fifty people died in Harper under extraordinary circumstances between 1952 and 1979. These are the people we know about. There could be more. None of the disappearances or deaths have ever been adequately explained. Law enforcement and medical professionals have time and again come to know the limits of their knowledge and the inadequacy of their prized rationality.

Regardless of the detente Harper seems to be locked in for the time being, regardless of how long it lasts, every Harperite who lived through these events will take the horror to their grave. For those who are bitter, their bitterness will also lie with them as the clenched hands of loved ones release and pour one final handful of dirt upon their caskets. Mrs. Neigh went to such a grave in 1989. Her life after the death of her son was not a life.

The death of Detective Ronald Chandler and his wife Veronica in 1978 at the hands of their own little boy shocked the entire community and left both my father and I without friends who had accepted us despite our stigmatized status in Harper. Paul Chandler had seen and heard something that I would not wish upon anyone. His father had already seen things which he couldn't find a logical answer for. And yet, he would not believe his son when he told him that he was forced to do what the wolfman thing ordered him to do.

Rodney Gilcairn's parents divorced and moved away from Harper and from California. To my knowledge, they never got their son's body back. I don't believe they ever got the answers they had been seeking for years. Even today letters to both the government and the city seeking information about what was responsible for the deaths of Rick Neigh and Rodney Gilcairn in 1977 go unanswered. Neither the government nor the city of Harper seem to have any answers.

The 12th Street Preschool and Kindergarten closed down in 1980. The two women who had put their hearts and souls into creating a nurturing and safe place for children to learn and grow had themselves grown tired of remembering. They no longer wished to be reminded of that fateful day in September, 1970 when they simply couldn't protect the three children who were entrusted to their care and who were brutally taken from this world by organisms with no name – creatures which simply should not exist.

Ironically, no newspaper clippings exist which describe the true nature of the events of July 2nd, 1979. More than thirty people saw a creature so violent and terrible that not even the cruelty that humans are capable of could compare. The senseless carnage and death caused by this humanoid miscreant still creates enough fear today to silence even those Harperites who want to understand why this happened, yet are afraid that it will return.

Rod's Big Burger still exists today. The diner that once united families and created a childhood atmosphere I will never forget also served as a testing ground in terror which those present on that day will never forget. But Rod's is stubborn in its continuity. Like so many Harperites, it hasn't changed. The furniture is still the same as it was during the 1950's and the mid-century flowerbeds are still there. The only thing that changed was the lives of the hostages. Most of them moved away from Harper after the incident.

My grandparents were among those present that day who later moved away. Grandpa and Grandma Ahnus did pull up and sell out. They moved to Laguna Beach and bought a large house upon a steep terraced hill where they had a magnificent view of the ocean. I frequently visited them. We would sit for hours together on a bench on Mountain Street overlooking the sea. There we would talk about togetherness and the times that were. We would try to comprehend how the things we experienced in Harper could have happened and whether they had changed us for the better or for the worse. We couldn't say which. But we all agreed that Harper had changed us.

Grandpa Ahnus passed away in 1987 and Grandma Ahnus followed her husband in 1990. They died of natural causes. They deserved that dignity and in Laguna Beach they had it. My sister Marina had two children and moved to Italy. We don't have that much contact anymore.

194

My father and mother divorced in 1990. Leida, my mother, was psychologically destroyed by what she had experienced in Harper. She is not unlike thousands of others in that city. Gareth, my father, lives most of the time on a large yacht which is moored at Dana Point. This was always one of his dreams, and after he left Harper it came true.

He and I would take the yacht out of Dana Point and sit talking for hours while the seagulls tried to drown out our words. The water would lap up against the yacht and we would laugh together at whatever there was left of our history in Harper to laugh about. My father had a policy of his own – he wanted to forget about the things in Harper and what he learned from his police friend. We would therefore hardly ever broche the subject.

In 1964 Esther Riina Tamm was pregnant. She and her family were initially ecstatic about the pending birth. Their child would be born a US citizen, just like Patrick had been. But word had reached the Tamm family about Soviet agents who were infiltrating Estonian exile organizations and actively hunting down defectors.

The Tamm's had always told Trisha that she should take Patrick and hide if anything suspicious ever happened to her parents. They told Trisha to deny their family relationship if the parents were captured and returned to Soviet Estonia. Trisha always said that she would never deny her parents and would go with them and meet the same fate if necessary.

When they heard this the Tamms spoke to Grandpa and Grandma Ahnus and tried to hatch a plan where the Ahnus family would claim to be Trisha's grandparents and state that they had a daughter in Canada. Clearly this was a half-baked and disingenuous plan. Even Priit and Esther Tamm began to admit this to themselves.

At one of those family gatherings at Rod's Big Burger my father was so touched by the horror of what could happen to the Tamms that he made a suggestion. Why not give the child up for adoption to an American citizen? he had proposed. That way, the child would also have US citizen parents who could keep the child in the United States. At first the Tamm's were ecstatic about the idea. But then the thought became painful to them.

If they gave the child away to an American couple, they would never see it again and the child would not even know that it was Estonian. My adopted mother thought long and hard about having another child to be responsible for. She already had Marina. And it was almost too much for her psychologically.

"Aga näete, Leida, et oleme teie kõrval!" (But you see, Leida, we'll be right next door!) Esther Tamm would allay my adopted mother's apprehensions. And so finally she agreed.

In 1965 both families approached the court explaining the unique situation and the danger the Tamm family might be facing. Given the atmosphere at the time and
196

the recentness of the Cuban Missile Crisis, the judge was very much onboard with the Tamm family's plans. It would be a sealed adoption and both families could reveal the fact per their agreement to the child once the child had reached adulthood. That family meeting never happened, for reasons which should be apparent.

In February of 1994 my adoptive mother received a letter from the Estonian embassy. It was actually addressed to me. Trisha Tamm had informed them about the adoption and about what had happened to our parents. The Estonian government was making restitution for and returning property to owners and heirs who had had their property stolen by the Communist regime. Trisha was not capable of taking care of the paperwork because she was in mental health care. But she wanted me to know who my real parents were and to have half of the family estate. That's how I found out.

I now knew why my hair is jet black – and was turning grey already when I reached thirty. The cat-eyes my late friends would tease me about now had an origin in the strawberry blonde family man I always thought was just a neighbor. Now, I believe I know why Patrick would constantly spy on me from over the creosote wood fence of my adoptive grandparents' back yard. They were all watching me – watching me grow, learn, hurt, laugh and live. And they knew I was safe.

As the years passed, I began to crave information about who had taken them away from me. Who was Clay? Was she a Soviet agent, just as my adoptive grandparents had feared? I would lay awake wondering. Had the disappearance of my parents been staged? Was it natural or supernatural? I kept deliberating.

In 2004 I traveled to Estonia and spoke to relatives, ministries, archives and even a retired KGB agent who knew what was happening during the 1960's. While the KGB and GRU did try to lure defectors and family members back to the Soviet Union through the use of relatives living in Estonia, none of my relatives had been asked to do this. The fate of my parents and brother terrified even the hardened and retired KGB agent.

There were no archives that could produce an explanation for what had happened to Priit, Esther and Patrick Tamm in 1972. Everyone I spoke with considered it highly unlikely that the KGB or GRU would have dispatched agents to capture or threaten my parents. They were simply – as the retired KGB agent had bluntly put it – not important enough.

When I returned from Estonia, my attention also turned to the American authorities. What did the FBI know? I asked myself with an urgency and panic. Had they learned anything after all of these decades? I wondered. When I finally met with a field agent in Los Angeles, I was furious. The agent went on about how I officially was not the Tamms' son and was not a party to the case.

Yet, the agent apparently could sense my rage and my hurt at not knowing what had happened to my parents and my brother. She told me that the case had been highly unusual and that the FBI had never before had such a case. They simply didn't have any answers.

Then I visited my sister Trisha at the Institute for Near Mental Care in Toronto. I saw before me – after more than thirty-five years – an old and wrinkled lady with grey hair who looked slightly like my mother. This was my biological older sister. And she still had the letters from our mother – the letters which had put her into a panic in 1972. Trish's doctor wouldn't let her have the letters personally for health reasons, so Trisha let me take them. And I read them.

What I read in the few lines our mother wrote in those letters has caused me to cry and to tremble with fear. Esther Tamm spoke of a "being" that had come to them as a woman asking for a place to stay and a job taking care of the house and Patrick. They had taken in her in. But Patrick knew who and what she was. They had met before – on a terrible day in early June.

They learned what Clay was and feared for their lives. It had taken them hostage and there was absolute nothing they could do. They knew that it would find them however far they tried to flee. There was nowhere they could hide from it. And there was no earthly power that could protect them from it.

All Esther Tamm could do was to warn her daughter not to try to intervene – for her own safety. Clay also knew I was Priit and Esther's son. It knew how to threaten the Tamms with that information too. And it had threatened to come calling for me at a later time. They had begged it not to.

As I imagine before me the little red note that Clay had left with the telescope, I now perceive its true meaning. There was no other point than to wait for the day that I would discover who Priit, Esther and Patrick were, and to know how much the knowledge of what had happened to them would then torment me. And that, dear reader, is how I came to believe in true goodness. For if true evil like this can exist, then true goodness certainly must as well.

CHAPTER 10   Epilogue

More creative works by this author

https://itunes.apple.com/us/artist/gunnar-k.-a.-njalsson/id49247270

http://spacepol.aero

CPSIA information can be obtained
at www.ICGtesting.com
Printed in the USA
LVHW09s2344230918
591144LV00001B/12/P